''I'm hallucinating!''

Her mouth was open, but Virginia couldn't do a thing about it. All she could do was stare at the vision before her—a little man in a bright green tunic, red tights and pointy-toed slippers.

She turned to Nick. "You don't see what I see, do you? It's me. My brain is frostbitten."

"Looks like an elf to me," Nick said lightly.

Virginia groaned. "Oh, Lord, we've both lost our grip on reality!"

The creature jumped up and, in one arcing leap, landed feather-light in the clearing between them. "Oh, no. I'm quite real. Most assuredly real."

Virginia swayed, as if to faint.

"No need to panic, Virginia," the little man said. "I've come to take you to Kris Kringle!"

Dear Reader,

Most of the year, I'm a pretty hardheaded, no-nonsense kind of person. Just ask my husband. He's the romantic one in the family, and I'm the one who checks my list to make sure I can make up the time later in the week if we take the afternoon off for a picnic.

But come December, I believe in magic.

I believe in the magic of snowflakes on your nose. I believe magic smells like cloves and cinnamon, tastes like homemade fudge and sounds like a choir of children singing "O Holy Night." It feels like the tears collecting in your eyes during the final scene of *It's a Wonderful Life*.

Well, I'm no Jimmy Stewart, but I wanted to do something to bring together the two most powerful forms of magic I know—Christmas and love. I hope you'll enjoy *Yes, Virginia*.... And I hope when you finish it, you'll know, as I do, that all you have to do is believe....

Happy holidays. I wish you love and peace.

Peg

Peg Sutherland

Peg Sutherland

YES, VIRGINIA...

Harlequin Books

TORONTO • NEW YORK • LONDON
AMSTERDAM • PARIS • SYDNEY • HAMBURG
STOCKHOLM • ATHENS • TOKYO • MILAN
MADRID • WARSAW • BUDAPEST • AUCKLAND

ISBN 0-373-16514-5

YES, VIRGINIA...

Copyright © 1993 by Peg Robarchek.

Prologue

A right jolly old elf . . .

"Bah, humbug!"

Kris snapped his red suspenders impatiently and turned away from the window. Elsa looked up from her crockery bowl of gingerbread batter. "Why, Kris! What a thing to say!"

Kris paced the cozily warm kitchen. A fire blazed in the stone fireplace, and the smell of sugar and spice radiated from the cast-iron stove built into the wall.

"I mean it. I'm tired of it. All of it!" He pushed his wire-rimmed glasses up on his button nose and scowled at the rosy-cheeked woman whose generous bosom was dusted with flour and cinnamon. "I'm tired of the toys. Tired of looking out the window and seeing nothing but snow. I'm tired of wearing red and I'm tired of checking that blasted list twice every year!"

Drawing her lips into a fussy pucker, Elsa walked around the massive kitchen table to take his hands in hers. "I thought that part was easier, now that it's all on computer."

"It is. It is. But...I'm getting too old for this, that's all." He huffed out a frustrated sigh, squared his shoulders and looked his wife straight in her twinkling blue eyes. "Let's retire, Elsa. Let's make this the last year."

Elsa smiled indulgently and put her arm around his shoulders. "Now, Kris, you know you always get exhausted this time of year. Why don't you have a nap this afternoon? Let Noel inspect the bicycles while you get some rest."

Kris suppressed the irritable protest threatening to surface. This wasn't Elsa's fault, and there was no reason to take it out on her—which was just one more part of the problem. He was sick and tired of being so gosh-darned jolly all the time! Four hundred years of being a jolly old elf would set anyone's teeth on edge. Some days he wanted to break every candy cane that came off the assembly line, just to prove he could be as cantankerous as anyone else.

But this wasn't his cantankerousness speaking now. "I'm serious, Elsa. Let's retire."

She stepped back, her pale eyes growing as wide and round as the midnight sun in July. "You mean this, Kris?"

For the first time that afternoon, Kris smiled. She was still the prettiest woman he'd ever met, with her big blue eyes and those dimples right at the corner of her mouth and the soft white waves framing her plump pink face. Remembering all the years she'd stood by his side and shared the load, he took her gently by the hand and led her to the window.

"Look, Elsa. What do you see?"

She leaned against him, settling her plump curves against his rounded belly in the way that always made him feel as warm as an oven full of her gingerbread cookies.

"Why, it's snow, Kris. You know that."

So it was. Acres and acres of snow. Miles of snow. Snow so bright and unending that even now, in the middle of an Arctic winter night, it glistened so brightly and crisply the moonlight might well have been sunshine. The vast white expanse was broken only by the bright peppermint-striped buildings scattered across the landscape, buildings that even now were bustling with the sound of welding and riveting and hammering and painting.

"Now, use your vision for a minute, Elsa, and imagine that it isn't snow at all," he whispered, already taken by the image that had been haunting him for weeks. "Imagine that it's sand. White, silvery sand. And that wind you hear roaring out there, Elsa, that's not wind at all. That's the ocean. Hear it, Elsa? Can you see the palm trees? Can you feel the sunshine, Elsa?"

"Oh, Kris."

She snuggled closer and sighed happily.

"That's Florida, Elsa. Wouldn't you like to retire to Florida, Elsa? Before we're too old to enjoy it?"

She brushed her nose against his snowy beard and rested her hand softly on his red flannel shirt. Kris closed his eyes and held her there, letting his daydream wash over them both. Then he chuckled softly. "You'll be a killer in a bikini, Elsa."

With a soft grunt, she pushed him away. Her smile faded quickly as she looked him in the eye. "But the children, Kris. What about the children?"

Kris smiled and touched her cheek. "Don't you think I've thought of that? I wouldn't just walk away. I've been looking."

"Looking?"

"For a replacement."

"A replacement?" Astonishment transformed her usually placid face.

"Why, sure, a replacement. It can be done."

"But who? Not just anybody could do what you do."

Kris sniffed the air. "Elsa, I think your first batch is ready."

With a startled cry, Elsa snatched up her oven mitt and yanked open the door. The smell of gingerbread filled the air as she pulled a long metal tray from the rack and set it out to cool. "Oh, dear. Oh, dear, I think they're overcooked. They'll be hard, Kris. Now look what you've made me do."

"They'll be perfect, Elsa. They always are."

When she looked up at him, he saw tears glistening on her eyelashes. "I suppose you think just anyone can make twelve million gingerbread people every year and have them come out perfect."

"Of course not. But I have someone in mind for you, too. You'll like her, Elsa."

She shook her head in disbelief. "You've already been searching. You didn't say a word and you've already been searching."

Kris grabbed a spare spatula and started loosening the aromatic cookies from the pan. "Wait till you meet them, Elsa. He's a good-looking cuss—reminds me of me in my youth, rather dashing, if I do say so myself. Spends his summers slashing through the jungle, leading expeditions. I'll bet you thought that kind of thing went out of style years ago, didn't you, Elsa? Oh, but he doesn't do it just for adventure, you understand. He's one of these save-the-rain-forest fellows, always leading scientists and environmentalists and that sort of thing. Why, he spent two years with the Akuchti, so I know he can stand the cold. Say, he fought an alligator once bare-handed—has the nick in his forearm to this day."

Elsa studied him carefully, her own spatula forgotten in the fist propped on her hip. "Two years with the Akuchti Eskimos is fine, Kris. But what about the children? Don't forget the children."

His smile was satisfied and confident. "I wouldn't forget that, Elsa. He's one of my unofficial helpers. Starts in September every year, making toys for the less fortunate little ones." He watched, gratified, as the cloud in his wife's eyes cleared somewhat with that news. "Grew up in one of those families where nobody had time for the kids. It's like a mission of his, seeing that kids don't do without."

"I see." Doubt still hovered in Elsa's eyes. She shook a finger at him. "But you know, Kris, it doesn't all rest on your shoulders. You need a strong woman at the helm. Someone who isn't afraid to cook from scratch."

Kris smiled so broadly his eyes almost disappeared behind his plump red cheeks. "Ah, Elsa, she's a jewel. Lost her mom and dad at a tender age. Lots of foster homes. A sad business, really. All she's ever wanted is a family." He shook his head forlornly. "And I've never quite been able to deliver, Elsa. You know how that kind of failure frustrates me. But she does love children. Wants lots of them."

Elsa chuckled and gave him a look he understood well. No one knew what it was to have lots of children to provide for until they'd been in Kris and Elsa's shoes for a year or two.

At that moment the kitchen door swung open, and Noel popped into the room, his color high and the bell on the end of his striped stocking cap jingling merrily.

"The bikes are ready, Kris! Wait till you see! Neon colors—they'll be a megahit!" In a few spry steps he was beside Elsa at the huge wooden table, standing on tiptoe to sniff the just-baked cookies.

"Ah, Elsa! You're a genius. An artist."

Still staring uncertainly at Kris, she shook her head. "Overcooked. They won't be good this year, I'm afraid."

"I could sample," Noel said. "You want me to sample, just to be sure?"

When he received her approving nod, Noel completed yet another annual ritual. He waited for Elsa to take her spatula and lift a cookie off the sheet. Then he nibbled tentatively at a foot, frowning in concentration as he then devoured a leg. And an arm. Soon the unadorned gingerbread person had disappeared. Noel licked a crumb from the corner of his lips and nodded.

"Perfect. Once again, Elsa. Perfect." Then she leaned over for the quick peck he always planted on her cheek. "You want me to sample the next batch, you just call."

Kris grunted. "And soon you'll be as plump as me."

Noel laughed, setting his bell atinkle. "So, are you ready for the annual bicycle inspection?"

Kris sighed and started for the door, but Elsa caught him by the arm and smiled the shy smile that had warmed countless Arctic winters for Kris.

"You really think…that is…about the bikini…?"

Glancing at Noel, who was preoccupied with dipping his finger in a near-empty bowl of gingerbread dough, Kris patted the generous swell of her hip. "You'll knock 'em dead."

She drew a long breath. "Okay. If you're really sure..."

With her words, Kris felt as if he had suddenly dropped an enormous burden he'd been lugging around on his back for centuries. He grabbed her and planted a grateful kiss on her forehead. "Ah, Elsa, you don't know what this means to me!"

His voice heartier than it had been in days, Kris turned to his assistant. "Noel, before we do that inspection, I need your help with one little project."

Licking the last of the dough from his index finger, Noel followed Kris out of the kitchen. "Okay, boss. Shoot."

"That newfangled fax machine. I want you to send a message for me." He pulled a sheet of paper out of his roomy pants pocket and unfolded it. "To the editor of the *Snowridge Daily Chronicle,* in Snowridge, Colorado."

Noel took the paper, nodded and headed toward Kris's office, reading the message as he went. Two steps away from the office door, he stopped and turned back to Kris, a distressed frown on his pointy little face. "Bossman, what the heck is this?"

"Your language, Noel. Watch your language. You know how Elsa feels about harsh language."

"But this is a want ad, Kris. You aren't... I mean, you can't..."

"Just testing the waters, Noel. Sending up a...what is it they say? A trial balloon, as it were. Nothing to worry about. Now, hurry, we've got bikes coming off the assembly line."

Noel turned slowly toward the office, then paused in his tracks once again. "What about... how do you think...?"

Kris knew what prompted Noel's reluctance. No one at the compound liked to be reminded of the treachery, but everyone found it hard to forget. So, in spite of the slight unease that Noel's reminder caused him, Kris smiled a cheery smile and said in his jauntiest voice, "Don't you worry about Theodore. No, sir. Theodore won't be a problem. Not for a minute."

Chapter One

He spoke not a word,
but went straight to his work....

Men like Nick Closthaler really gave Virginia Holley a pain in the caboose.

Spare me from the strong, silent type, she thought as she watched his broad hands play over the pile of boards at his elbow, selecting one that pleased him.

Not that she didn't understand what he was do-ing—she did it herself whenever anyone threatened to get too close. But right now she had a job to do. And if Nick Closthaler continued to clamp his jaws shut, the glare from those penetrating gray eyes daring her to do a darn thing about it... well, he simply didn't know Virginia Holley.

As if he could intimidate her simply because she was only a wood shaving over five feet tall. Simply be-cause she looked like a blond, blue-eyed baby doll with dimples at the corners of her mouth.

Virginia felt herself steaming up. Yes, men like Nick always seemed to think they could manipulate cute little Virginia Holley. Simply because they were taller, with big barrel chests and thick patches of hair curling up from the necks of their flannel shirts and a two-day growth of beard gracing their chins. Simply because they looked and sounded like he-men, and she looked and sounded like Doris Day stuck in terminal adolescence.

Virginia wanted to clobber him with her Nikon, catch him with the business end of her wide-angle lens, right on the crown of the bright red knit cap covering his salt-and-pepper curls. After all, she had been perfectly pleasant to him after trudging up the side of this godforsaken mountain. And she wasn't exactly out to fry his liver for lunch, for pete's sake.

"It's a simple Christmas feature story," she started once again, refusing to wheedle but nevertheless relying heavily on the little-girl timbre of her voice. Well, if she could turn an obvious shortcoming to her advantage, why the heck not? "You know, one of those schmaltzy, tear-in-your-eye deals. *It's a Wonderful Life* on page one."

The man named Nick barely looked at her, but as his eyes glanced at her face, Virginia felt herself...what, growing warm? Soft inside? She gave herself a mental kick for being a sap. Now disgruntled at herself, too, she did her best to keep it out of her voice.

"You know, just to remind everybody that Christmas is about more than lines at the cash register and credit-card meltdowns."

It looked hopeless. She'd known right away she was in trouble, the minute she'd introduced herself as a reporter from the *Snowridge Daily Chronicle*, then waited for a full ninety seconds while Nick Closthaler ignored her outstretched hand.

Still ignoring her, Nick positioned a template on the straight, knot-free board he had selected and penciled in the outline of a train engine. Giving herself a moment to maintain her calm, Virginia raised her camera and clicked off another shot of him at work.

"We've heard the children in Sugarplum Bluff have adopted you as sort of an unofficial Santa Claus, Mr. Closthaler," she had said after he shunned her handshake, tilting her head to allow the sun to highlight her freckles. Anything to make him realize she wasn't here with a film crew from "60 Minutes." "We think that's a story worth sharing with our readers."

He had stared at her, his gray eyes darkening to pewter, the furrow between his brows deepening. But even with several days' worth of stubble on his ruddy cheeks, even though his square chin easily topped her fuzzy white hat, Virginia wasn't afraid of him. Even up here, miles from town, several hundred feet and a narrow path above her four-wheel drive Jeep, where she couldn't hope to get to safety—or even civilization—in less than forty-five minutes, she found nothing in Nick Closthaler that alarmed her. And she had learned young that she could trust her gut instincts.

"I don't have time for that," he had said at last, then pushed past her abruptly and stalked across his front yard to the tumbledown building that had turned out to be his workshop. A stroke of good fortune, as far as Virginia was concerned.

She had trotted after him, pulling her notebook out of her camera bag.

"I understand," she had said cheerfully, looking around and making note of the fact that the only product of his workshop seemed to be toys. "You must be busy this time of year. I would've called, but you've got no phone. The folks down in Sugarplum Bluff said the only way to reach you was to come up."

She had thought it prudent not to mention that every single adult she had questioned about him had made a point of telling her to stay away from the village's most eccentric recluse.

"But I won't get in your way. I'll just sit by while you work, ask a few questions and take a few notes. Okay?"

Even as she spoke, she was taking notes. The tools he used. What he was wearing. Every physical impression she could quickly register to add flavor to her feature. She might hate this kind of sentimental drivel, but she would still do a bang-up job.

"No."

The single word had sunk in as she was admiring the stack of old-fashioned unpainted sleds piled under the worktable. She turned back to him and was surprised to find him standing so close. So close her breath caught in her throat.

My, he is a big one.

"I beg your pardon?" She wanted to bite nails when she realized she sounded a little breathless. She wasn't living up to the no-nonsense, professional image she liked to project. Not at all.

"You should leave. I don't want a story."

That hadn't fazed Virginia. Almost everyone said that at first. So she had cajoled. She had explained, over and over again, that her motives were strictly pure and in the spirit of the season—which was at least marginally true. She had tried easing in a question here and there, all the while clicking off a roll of film as unobtrusively as possible.

Nothing had budged Nick Closthaler. He was a mountain. A big, solid stone mountain that she could neither move nor step around.

And now, exactly forty-two minutes after meeting him, she would gladly give him a black eye with her reporter's pad.

Except, of course, that would never get the story. And get the story she would. Even if it meant showing this undomesticated man exactly how much power dimples and blue eyes could wield.

"Mr. Closthaler, let's forget about the children here in Sugarplum Bluff for a minute." Who knows? Maybe he was just shy about being such a do-gooder. But every woman knew that no man could resist a little ego stroking.

With her most persuasive smile, she eased closer to the workbench, where Nick was guiding a hunk of wood through a jigsaw. It was coming out the other end shaped remarkably like an old-fashioned steam engine. Virginia made a note in her pad without looking down, hoping her action wouldn't distract him. "I understand you're actually quite an adventurer, too. Exploring. Mountain climbing. How daring!"

He glanced up at her from beneath his stern, unruly eyebrows, those steely eyes once again issuing a warning Virginia had no intention of heeding. And once again he didn't speak. He simply finished pushing the wood through the saw, then held it up for inspection. He felt the edge of the cut he'd just made with the pad of his thumb, which Virginia noticed looked powerful and callused, like the rest of his big, square hand. He squinted and looked closer at the raw wood, blew away the sawdust clinging to it and finally set it aside on his worktable, next to another equally raw train engine. Behind the table were shelves of trains and planes and spaceships in various stages of completion, from sanded white pine to brightly painted and varnished.

"I understand your last adventure made a convert of a CEO whose company had a horrendous environmental record. Tell me how that came about."

"None of your business," Nick Closthaler said, simply and with no discernible animosity, as he clicked off the jigsaw and swung a powerful leg over the bench he'd been straddling.

Virginia bit down on the insides of her mouth to squelch the retort festering there. Instead, she looked up at him with the baby blues that historically melted anything in a jockstrap and smiled again, this time more coaxingly than the last.

"I can appreciate your not wanting any credit for what you do for these children, Mr. Closthaler," she said, wondering if now was the time to reach out and place her hand suppliantly on his arm. She found the idea of touching that flannel-clad biceps appealing in a disturbingly physical way. She decided to play that card only if necessary. "But what you do is special. What you do... why, it embodies the true spirit of Christmas. It..."

Virginia was ready to gag on her own words, but she was nevertheless surprised when Nick's resonant voice interrupted her.

"It's time for you to leave, Miss Holley."

Then he turned and walked out of the shop and into the cool mountain air.

The instant Virginia realized she was standing alone in the middle of his pine-scented workshop with her mouth hanging open, she shoved her notebook into the pocket of her ski jacket, clamped her teeth tightly together and stalked out after him.

The view from the path outside his shop almost took her breath away and left her gaping once again. Perched high on one of the many bluffs and peaks ringing the tiny village of Sugarplum Bluff, Nick Closthaler's homesite was as close to heaven as Virginia could ever remember being. Through the stand of towering pines and blue spruces, she could see the vivid green hillside sloping down to the little town, which was picturesquely dotted with stone homes and rough-hewn lodges. Across the sun-dappled valley, the slopes rose again, ending in sheer Rocky Mountain peaks, their cragginess muted by snow much of the year.

From here the view belonged to Nick Closthaler, a recluse who—when he wasn't out risking his neck at the macho adventuring the villagers had mentioned—spent his time holed away in a tiny, hand-built cabin. His only transportation was by skis or snowshoes. His only friends were the children of the village, whose faces lit up like Christmas trees when his name was mentioned.

You'll have to dredge up better prose than that when you get back to the Chronicle *and start writing this dog of a story,* Virginia chastened herself as she turned away from the view and continued her pursuit of the story she had been assigned.

She reached his front door just as it was thudding closed behind Nick. The first push she gave it didn't budge the massive slab of wood, so she gave it the mightiest shove her one-hundred-and-two-pound frame could manage and entered Nick's sanctuary.

The single room surprised Virginia as much as the stubborn streak she had encountered when trying to interview Nick. She had been in enough "rustic" Colorado cabins to know that most of them were self-consciously decorated in one trendy style or another. There was the ultrachic, the New Age western, the smoked-glass modern, the determinedly mountain. All gave Virginia a twinge in her phony detector.

Nick's cabin was none of those.

Nick's cabin was stark. The walls were bare. The plank floors were bare. The only furniture was a small, hand-hewn table accompanied by a matching straight-back chair and a large, hand-carved bed topped with a feather mattress and two quilts, both frayed and faded but bold in color and texture. Nick sat on a three-legged wooden stool beside the stone fireplace that made up one wall of the cabin. He poured himself a mug of whatever was in the black iron kettle that hung over the smoldering logs.

"Are you going to throw me out?" she asked, crossing the room to stand squarely in front of him. The fluttering-eyelash routine hadn't worked, which pleased Virginia in some perverse way. Time to get hard-nosed about this.

"I might."

"How about some hot tea first?" She rubbed her gloved hands together. "It's cold out there."

He stared back at her from across the top of his oversize pottery mug. She wasn't certain, but for a moment she thought she saw the glint of humor in his eyes before he lowered them to his cup again. With one big hand, he loosened the wool scarf at his neck as he swallowed.

She had been right. The curls rose up, dense and dark, from the V of his flannel shirt. They brought an inexplicable and unwanted rush of breath to her throat.

He bent to set his cup on the stone hearth, reaching for a long-handled cup of dented metal hanging from a hook on the hearth. He filled it with steaming tea and held it out to her.

"You'll have to use the dipper. It's all I've got."

Surprised into silence by this inadvertently revealing fact, Virginia was suddenly struck by a feeling all reporters know—the compulsion to find out more, to discover all there was to discover. No visitors? No friends? No pals in to watch the Super Bowl? Whatever he might be, Nick Closthaler was no ordinary do-gooder.

"I didn't ask to do this story, Mr. Closthaler." She made her voice pleasant but firm as she took the dipper, pulled up the chair he hadn't offered and sat to face him. "But it isn't as if we're out to do some big exposé. It's a simple holiday feature, one of those feel-good pieces that boosts everybody's holiday spirit and—"

"You're repeating yourself, Miss Holley. And it won't do any good. I'll serve the holiday spirit in my own way." He was no longer looking her directly in the eye. He was staring into the cup in his hands; Virginia was consumed with the need to find out what made him tick, and the fear that it would never happen. "I don't need your newspaper to do that."

"You're right. But we need you." The last time Virginia could remember such a reluctant interview subject was the failed savings-and-loan board member with the two-million-dollar mountain chalet. Her reporter's skepticism, which usually hibernated when she was on one of these puff pieces, clicked on.

What does Nick Closthaler have to hide? she wondered. Because everybody has something—that was her belief.

Even me.

"Find someone else with a story to tell," he said softly.

Virginia understood. Nick Closthaler would never tell his story. And she had to respect that. After all, she had never willingly told hers, either.

Still, she had a job to do. She stood and left her cup on the table. And she played the last card all good reporters played, knowing instinctively it wouldn't change Nick Closthaler's mind in the least.

"I'll get the story, Closthaler. I'll get it from the people in the village. I'll get it from the children." She zipped her ski jacket and hefted her camera bag to her shoulder. "It might not turn out the way you'd like it, but I'll get the story."

Then she turned and walked out.

She was halfway down the steep, rocky path to her Jeep when she realized that she was more disappointed at not being able to crack Nick Closthaler than she had been when she couldn't quite nail the S&L slimeball.

What the heck, you never get what you really want for Christmas anyway. Right?

NICK PROPPED his elbows on his knees and told himself the big, flat rock near the bottom of the ridge right outside the village was a great place to watch the annual burning of the Yule bonfire.

The square was aswarm with people, all bundled up for warmth and busy lugging dead limbs and other debris from the nearby woods to the village square. A Main Street merchant handed out cups of steaming hot chocolate. Another passed out candles. Everyone looked merry. Festive. The children in particular couldn't keep still, they were so excited.

Despite the numbness settling into his joints from the cold and the unyielding surface of the rock, Nick found the view acceptable. Whenever he was home, he watched most of the community activities from here—the Easter sunrise service, the spring-thaw parade, the fireworks on Independence Day. He enjoyed the festivities the way he enjoyed the harvest festivals in South America and the planting rituals in Asia and the coming-of-age celebrations in Africa.

Well, not exactly the way he enjoyed these. In those far-flung parts of the world, he was an outsider by birth. Here he was an outsider by choice.

There he felt happy in his role as observer. Here, well, the best that could be said was that he had accepted that role.

He watched as the people of Sugarplum Bluff held candles over their song sheets and sang carols. Their voices floated up to him, sounding rich and melodious through the grace of distance. He especially enjoyed the faces of the children, almost all of whom he knew. Their faces were filled with wonder, with excitement, with anticipation, with the magic of knowing the impossible *can* happen, even if only at this time of year. He liked doing his part to keep that magic alive; he knew firsthand what childhood was like when the magic died.

Then his roaming eyes lighted on what he had been seeking.

Virginia Holley.

Her hair was like a halo of moonlight around her face, a face as round and innocent as some of the children's. Fair and petite, she stood apart from the crowd, watching with a wistfulness that was unsettlingly familiar to Nick. Yet for all the vulnerability he read in her face and eyes, she also had a look of invincibility about her. In sturdy jeans and serviceable ski jacket, she showed him none of the vanity or pretension he had come to mistrust in women. She walked purposefully, stood solidly, looked around her with confidence. Occasionally she pulled her hands out of her pockets to write something in the notebook she kept shoved into her camera bag. He remembered how tiny those hands had been and how compelled he had been to take one of them in his own when she offered a handshake with her introduction.

Virginia Holley. He let the name echo in his mind, trying it out to see where it fit.

From this distance, even when people in the crowd set fire to the brittle tinder under the mass of wood and the Yule fire leapt into flame, Nick couldn't discern her freckles or those wide blue eyes. But he remembered them. They were burned into his mind's eye.

So much so that he had been frightened the minute she scampered over the top of the ledge to his homesite.

Frightened because that hadn't been the first time he'd seen her. For almost a week now, Nick had seen her every night. In his dreams. He wasn't certain what that might mean. He was only certain that her appearance in his life made him more uneasy than the worst dangers he had ever encountered in the world's most remote jungles.

Chapter Two

His eyes, how they twinkled....

Virginia tossed her camera bag, her notebook and her powder blue ski jacket onto her desk, threatening the precarious balance of clutter. Ignoring the imminent likelihood of a dangerous paper-slide, she marched through the near-empty newsroom and plopped herself in the swivel chair next to Oz Lundy.

"Ozzie, this is a dog," she announced, wondering just how much groveling it would take to convince the grouchy old city editor to trash-can the story on Nick Closthaler. "This guy in Sugarplum Bluff is no Santa Claus, trust me."

Oz leaned back in his chair and propped his feet on the edge of his computer stand. "So forget it."

"I'm telling you, he won't talk. Sure, we could talk to the kids, do the story any—" Her badgering skidded to a halt. "What?"

"I said forget it."

"Oh." Giving in without bloodshed wasn't like Ozzie. Then Virginia spotted the glint in his eyes and the nervous little telltale twitch in his right cheek as he fingered the piece of paper in his hand. "What now, Ozzie?"

"I've got a better story for you."

He tossed the paper into her lap. She picked it up, darting one more glance at the wicked little gleam in the city editor's eyes before she read the type on the slick fax paper:

Wanted: Couple to replace retiring philanthropists and toy-makers. Seasonal job. Long hours. Love of children and tolerance for cold weather a must. Some air travel involved. Cleanshaven men need not apply. Apply in person to K.K., North Pole.

With a cynical chuckle, Virginia looked up. "Cute, Oz. So whose idea of a joke is this?"

Ozzie shrugged. "It was faxed into the classified department."

Virginia rolled her eyes. "This time of year, I thought all the crazies had enough to keep them busy. So what are you doing with it?"

"I'm not doing anything with it. You are."

"Very funny." She stood and tossed the fax onto his desk. "I get the message. I'll stay on Closthaler's tail."

Ozzie grabbed her hand and stuffed the fax back into it. "I'm not kidding, Holley. I want a story."

"Oh, come on, Oz," she protested. "What am I all of a sudden, on the holiday-nutcase beat?"

"Yeah, now that you mention it." And he guffawed as he took a just-off-the-press paper from a copy carrier. "Now, get outta my face, Holley. I got to see if any of you college kids we hire around here have landed us a lawsuit today."

"Ozzie, give me a break." She stood her ground while he turned his attention to the paper. "I'm hardly a college kid anymore. I'm a good reporter. You don't really want me wasting time on..."

"Get me the story and quit bellyaching about it," Oz snapped in the gruff voice that every reporter on the staff knew meant business. "I know it's fluff. People love that kind of junk at Christmas. Makes 'em cry in their eggnog. Now beat it before I get you to write the cutline for the photo of the kitten in the Christmas stocking."

Squeezing her eyes tightly shut, Virginia held the tension for a few moments, then let her face gradually ease back to normal as she muttered, "Relax and let go." When her eyes were fully open again, the first thing she spotted was the thinning spot at the crown of Ozzie's haircut. She realized her teeth were still clenched. "And don't ambush your boss."

Resigned to being at the mercy of Ozzie's whims, Virginia walked back to her desk. As she began to restore some semblance of order to the mass of papers that had slithered off her desk and onto the floor, she tried to look on the bright side.

At least she would have something to think about besides Nick Closthaler. He had occupied entirely too many of her thoughts since she had spotted him hugging his knees and watching the Sugarplum Bluff Yule fire all alone in the shadows the night before. The sight of him, alone while everyone else celebrated, had tugged at her heart and stirred a longing she knew from experience was best left unexplored.

With visions of Nick dancing in her head, Virginia picked up the phone at her desk and rang the classified department. "Yeah, this is Holley in news. I need to talk to whoever pulled this fax from the crackpot with the Santa Claus fetish."

"ARE YOU really Santa Claus?"

Nick stood up from his workbench and stretched the kinks out of his back as he looked down at the young helper who had been handing him tools and generally supervising production.

"Now where'd you get that idea, Ethan?" Nick ruffled the youngster's carrot-colored hair.

Ethan shrugged, then looked up with a big grin that showed the space where a front tooth was missing. "The lady said so."

Nick knew without asking what lady. That pushy reporter who had run all over Sugarplum Bluff asking questions about him. He fought back a threatening frown and lifted Ethan, setting him on the edge of his worktable.

"Now listen here, young man, do you think I look like Santa Claus?" And he patted his stomach to point up what he hoped was a major difference between himself and the plump guy from the North Pole.

Ethan giggled. "No. You don't even have a beard...yet."

Nick rubbed his chin, which he kept meaning to shave. But a little extra covering was always welcome when winter blew in. "That's right. And I can't fly. I don't even have a reindeer."

"Wendy Hansel's dad said you used to live at the North Pole," Ethan challenged.

Nick couldn't help but wonder how so many people in the village knew so much about his private life. Except for the children, he didn't know any of them, and didn't associate with any of them. But as they did in small towns everywhere, he supposed, they had either uncovered or invented enough about Nick Closthaler to satisfy their curiosity.

"Well, not exactly at the North Pole. With the Akuchti. They're Eskimos."

Ethan's eyes grew wide. "Eskimos! Did you live in an igloo? And have a sled dog? Did you fight any polar bears, Nick?"

Nick laughed. "Tell you what. Let's get this workshop all cleared away, and I'll tell you about it over a bowl of chili. You getting hungry?"

"Gosh, yeah!"

For the next half hour, the two scurried around the workshop clearing up the clutter left by their morning of toy making. Shelf after shelf of bright, shining toys winked back at Nick and Ethan from all around the workshop. By the end of the day, Nick would have enough toys to provide a happy holiday for every needy child within a hundred-mile radius of Sugarplum Bluff.

And that meant he would have to find something else for Ethan or Wendy or Kevin to help him with the next time they made their way up the mountain. And they would be up. They wandered up to find him pretty regularly, drawn to him, he supposed, in the same way he was drawn to them. He was drawn by their innocence, their trust, their belief in him. And they were drawn to him, he supposed, because he did what he could to live up to their innocence, trust and belief.

Ethan wasn't one of the needy ones—at least not one of the ones who would need his toys. He was more needy, Nick knew, of his father's time. Ethan's family had plenty of money, but not much time for a seven-year-old. His dad was always busy with the electronics company that put money in the bank, furnished their mountain chalet and bankrolled their ski trips.

Actually, Nick knew from experience, Ethan needed even more than the kids whose only new toys would be the ones stacked up in his workshop.

"...how come the real Santa doesn't help?"

Nick realized he had been only half listening to Ethan's chatter as they scurried around the workshop sweeping up sawdust and putting tools in place. "What's that?"

"If you're not Santa Claus and you have to give toys to the poor kids, how come the real Santa doesn't help?"

Nick propped the push broom against the wall and took Ethan's small, soft hand in his. As he did, he was mindful of the trust he was guardian of when a seven-year-old brought him such a dilemma. The thought didn't frighten him; it merely swelled up in his heart and seemed to open up space for Ethan and others like him.

"Well, Ethan," he said carefully as they walked out the workshop door, "I guess you know there are a lot of poor kids in the world."

He looked down to catch Ethan's bright head bobbing up and down.

"So I guess you'd understand if Santa needed a little help?"

Ethan gave his big friend a skeptical look. "He's got elves for that."

Nodding, Nick squatted to look Ethan squarely in the eye. "That's true. Do you suppose all Santa's helpers live at the North Pole with him? Or do you suppose he might send some of them to live other places, so they'll be closer to the action?"

Ethan's eyes widened. He stared for a long moment, then spoke in a hushed whisper. "Are you one of the elves? Is that why you lived at the North Pole? Because you were in training? Wow, are there any more elves in Sugarplum Bluff? Wow!"

"Well, let's just say the old fellow in the red coat enlisted my help a long time ago." Suppressing a laugh, Nick clasped his hand on Ethan's shoulder and stood, drawing a deep breath of mountain air. "Now, how about some of that chili?"

With a shout of approval, Ethan scampered toward the cabin, leaving Nick standing at the edge of the ridge, surveying the valley. From where he stood, he could see the smoke curling out of many of the stark little houses he would visit in the weeks ahead. After quietly leaving his handiwork in the care of grateful parents, Nick always liked to imagine the little ones on Christmas morning. Freckles and pigtails and sleep-filled eyes grown suddenly alert. Dozens, he had seen to that first year. Then hundreds.

Then it had mushroomed, and providing Christmas for a few kids in Colorado hadn't seemed like enough. Like someone on a mission, he had badgered that schoolbook publisher into backing a project for educating the children in one of the villages where he'd spent time in Central America. That was a lot like Christmas, too. Suddenly there were hundreds more faces. Next he'd bullied his banker into supporting a scholarship project... and there must be a thousand faces by now.

But it wasn't enough.

This year something gnawed at him, goading him with the knowledge there was more to be done.

"Nick!" He looked toward Ethan, who now stood on the top step of the cabin. "Does that mean I'm a Santa's elf, too?"

Grinning, Nick closed the distance between them in a few long strides. "It's a big job, you know."

Ethan nodded solemnly.

"And you can't go bragging about it. True Santa's elves have to keep quiet."

Ethan looked distinctly disappointed. "You mean I can't tell everybody at school?"

"Then you wouldn't be a true Santa's helper."

Wrinkling his nose, Ethan considered the proposition. "Will I get extra toys if I'm a helper?"

"Not necessarily. You don't see a lot of extra toys in my house, do you?"

Now the little boy frowned. "Then what's the point?"

"Because it makes you happy to help other people be happy." He wondered, as he said it, if it were even true. Because it was beginning to feel as if he could never do enough to make people happy, as if he needed to do more and more and more before he could be satisfied.

"Oh."

"Like the time we shoveled snow for old Mrs. Norcroft. Remember how happy we felt when we saw how happy she was?"

"But she gave us cookies. And hot chocolate."

"That's true. But didn't you feel good before that? When she came out on the porch and smiled at us?"

Ethan thought a moment, then looked up and grinned. "Yeah! And she said it looked pretty as a picture, the way we smoothed it out next to her sidewalk instead of just piling it up."

"That's right. That's what being one of Santa's helpers is all about. So what do you think?"

"I could try."

"Good. Now, why don't you start by seeing if you can make Grover a little happier this morning." He pointed to the fat brown squirrel perched expectantly on the stump in the middle of the yard. The ground was still spotted with patches of snow that hadn't yet melted from the past week's fall.

While Ethan dashed to the bin where Nick kept his supply of nuts and seeds for the birds and squirrels, Nick again felt overwhelmed by the compulsion to do...something. Something he couldn't get a handle on. All he really knew was that this restlessness in him was all tied up with the woman who had come traipsing up the mountain wanting to know why he took care of the kids.

She ought to be out asking why everybody isn't taking care of the kids, he silently grumbled. Impatient with his thoughts, he watched as Ethan tossed a handful of nuts onto the snowy ground a few yards from the squirrel with the crook in his tail. When the offering hit the ground, Nick's unofficial pet took a graceful leap and landed beside it. *Why aren't we all taking care of the kids? That's the real story.*

But she wouldn't leave him alone. Oh, she hadn't made another trip up the mountain, but she kept coming back at him anyway, getting inside his head where he couldn't dismiss her quite so easily. She kept smiling at him, flashing those two little dimples that barely nicked the corners of her mouth, crinkling up those baby blue eyes, her pale, white blond curls dancing in the Colorado sunshine. She was taunting him.

Yes, somehow this Virginia Holley was the one who kept bringing him the message that he should be doing more. That the job wasn't as simple as he'd thought it was.

You're getting antsy, that's all, he told himself as he headed to his cabin to warm up the pot of chili. *Ready to get out of here, do something. Go somewhere.*

The rain forest was calling. That must be it. His January plans were already nibbling at him. He'd signed on to guide environmentalists deep into the rain forest. He was already feeling the excitement that accelerated his heart and rushed through his muscles the closer he got to one of his trips. He could already smell the dampness, the sweetness of the tropics.

At least, that's what he told himself.

But in truth another urge was calling more loudly. The urge of air so cold you had to breathe it through a wool scarf or risk freezing your throat and lungs; the urge of holding the tethers that commanded the strength and speed of a team of dogs; the urge of looking out over an expanse of endless isolation and blinding frigidity.

The urge of thousands—millions—of little faces who needed someone on their side. And one not-so-little face with probing eyes and a determined chin.

VIRGINIA WAS NEXT.

Yes, Virginia knew everyone was looking at her. She was the only adult without a child in the line waiting to see the old gentleman in the red suit. But she had tried to wheedle her way past the women taking the photos the last time this mall Santa was on break. Despite their precious red stocking caps and flared skating skirts, the two women had proved to be formidable bodyguards.

So Virginia had waited in line with all the tired, whining babies in buggies and the shy, thumb-sucking toddlers. She actually enjoyed the twenty minutes, time she spent anticipating the day when she would drag her own babies through a similar line.

That day would come, she assured herself as a toddler grabbed her finger with a sticky hand. Five of them, at least, she thought, with sticky fingers and socks that won't stay up. A permanent family. A big family. Really big.

So she was smiling when she arrived at the head of the line and marched toward the Santa with the real, snowy beard and the wire-rimmed glasses. Her smile deepened when she realized he was looking at her with an unmistakable twinkle in his dark eyes.

"Hi, Santa." She did, after all, feel a little foolish. But she was determined to talk to *this particular* Santa, the only one in town with a real beard and real white hair. "I'm with the *Chronicle* and..."

"Virginia, I believe."

"Yes, and..." She paused in the process of pulling her notebook out of her pocket and stared at him. Well, it wasn't as if people recognized her on a regular basis, but she supposed it could happen. "Right. Well, I'm working on a story and I wanted to ask you a couple of questions."

"I see. Well, don't you suppose you should sit on my knee?"

Even mall Santas with real beards could have a little streak of lechery in them, she supposed. She smiled and shook her head. "No, I don't think that'll be necessary."

The Santa looked troubled. "It's a little unorthodox otherwise, don't you agree?"

"Well..." She eased closer. He was awfully grandfatherly. She perched gingerly on his knee as she found the copy of the fax. "What I'm working on, I hate to even take your time. I know you're busy. And this is just a silly little holiday story, but..."

"Wouldn't you like to put in your Christmas order first?"

His voice, kindly and deep, stopped her, and she looked into his eyes again. She felt naked. Not in the way that new reporter on the staff had made her feel at the Halloween party a few weeks ago. But naked from the soul out. As if this old gentleman in the surprisingly authentic-looking red suit could actually see all the lonely Christmases in her past.

But even a Santa with a real beard couldn't grant the Christmas wish she had harbored for so many years. "Well, um..."

"It's perfectly all right, you know. I mean, you waited in line like everyone else."

"Yes, but..."

"Nonsense. Nothing's too tough for Santa."

She laughed, a nervous little laugh that sounded almost like a giggle to her. But his eyes held her mesmerized. And she knew even before she opened her mouth that she was powerless to stop herself from saying something foolish to this fake Kris Kringle.

"Okay, then. I want... a family."

He nodded. *He's really quite good,* she thought. *Very convincing.* "A big one, I presume?"

Her heart pounded a little harder at the thought, seemed to drop in her chest, the feeling like whizzing to the bottom of the steepest incline on a roller coaster. "Very big."

"One that won't... abandon you? Leave you all alone again?"

Virginia's hard-earned skepticism surfaced once again. She swallowed the lump in her throat. "Hey, who the heck are you, anyway?"

"I think I can arrange that." He nodded thoughtfully, ignoring her accusing question.

"You can?" Despite herself, she felt the wistful hope renewing itself.

"I believe so. But . . ."

Ah, this was the part where he weaseled out of it, of course. "But what?" she asked smugly.

"Well, you may get a bit more family than you bargained for. Would that be all right?"

The vision filled her head. Children. Laughter. Stockings hung from the chimney and little voices raised in an off-key rendition of "Silent Night." A family. It was a moment before Virginia realized that she was blinking hard to clear the moisture in her eyes. "Oh, Santa, you couldn't come up with a family too big for me."

And he surprised her by laughing right out loud, a big, booming laugh that was so infectious she joined him. And when his belly had stopped shaking and Virginia remembered why she was sitting on this mall Santa's knee, she handed him the fax in her hand.

"Oh, yes. Your story. Now, let's see, what's this?"

And he read while she got her pen and pad ready to record his comments. As she waited, he raised his spiky white eyebrows, frowned slightly and said, "Well, young lady, I must say this is a surprise to me."

Virginia smiled. "No memos from headquarters, then?"

"No, none. As a subordinate Claus, I haven't heard a word about this. Could start a panic, you know?"

At last, a good quote, Virginia thought. "Are you considering applying for the position?"

But he hardly seemed to notice her. He just kept shaking his head and frowning. "Oh, dear. Oh, gracious. I wonder if the union steward knows anything about this."

"The elves' union?"

"Yes, yes." He looked up, concern and determination in his eyes. "Excuse me, miss, but I really must see about this. You will excuse me?"

And without waiting for her reply, he placed his hands around her waist and lifted her off his knee. Then, ignoring the short-skirted photographers and the wails of protest rising up from parents who had waited in line interminably, he started walking away.

As she watched him retreat, Virginia did the most ridiculous thing she could remember doing in a long time. She chased after him, and putting her hand on his shoulder to stop him, she looked up into his no-longer-twinkling but still-kindly eyes and whispered, "You won't forget, will you?"

"Forget? Oh! The family. No. No, I won't forget."

Then he turned and walked away. All Virginia could do was watch him until he was out of sight. Finally she stuffed her notebook, her pen and the fax back into her pocket and walked out into the early December chill. All the way back to her car, she caught sight of mothers and their children and couldn't stop the little lift of foolish hope that she knew better than to acknowledge.

When she pulled her Jeep into a parking space outside the newsroom a few minutes later, hers was one of only three other vehicles in the lot. There was Ozzie's old yellow Cadillac with the fins, the rickety bike that belonged to the photo-lab boy, and the old but well-maintained sedan that belonged to the press-room foreman.

Once inside, she draped her jacket over the back of her desk chair and plopped down, waving to acknowledge Ozzie's greeting. Then she pulled her notebook out and propped the fax up against her row of dictionaries, the Associated Press stylebook and that old guide to grammar she used to defend herself against Ozzie's creative editing from time to time.

She had plenty of cute stuff. Quotes from parents— "Well, I certainly hope he doesn't expect *us* to do all the work next year!"—and from Santas. But, of course, nothing concrete, unless she could determine where the fax came from. Shaking her head, she looked at the header at the top of the fax sheet. No company name. Just the phone number. And this phone number was weird. Too many numbers, for starters.

Virginia picked up her phone, dialed the operator and asked where the number originated. Then she waited. And waited.

"Operator? Any luck?" she asked, trying to curb her impatience.

"Still checking," the voice in her ear said cheerfully.

So Virginia waited some more, using the time to make a list of the few gifts she needed to get this year.

Something for Ozzie, just because the old curmudgeon wouldn't expect it. And something for Mama Stephens, her sixth foster mother. She'd lived with her the year she had started junior high. And maybe a little something for the *Chronicle* switchboard operator, because she'd heard from Ozzie that Hettie was all alone in the world, and Virginia knew exactly how that felt, especially at this time of the year. And...

"North Pole."

Virginia snapped back to attention. "I beg your pardon?"

"That number is the North Pole."

"The North... What are you talking about?"

Virginia heard the operator draw a deep, patient breath. "The number you asked about, miss. That number is the North Pole."

"But..."

"Thank you for calling Mountain Bell, miss."

The operator disconnected the line.

Baffled, Virginia stared at the telephone in her hand until it started buzzing irritatingly at her. Then she replaced it and stared at the telephone number at the top of her fax. Then she did what any good reporter would do who doubted her facts. She called another operator. And waited again. Only to hear the same thing.

"That's the North Pole, ma'am."

And again. But nothing she did convinced the operators to tell her something reasonable. Even their supervisors repeated the same nonsense. Finally Virginia did what she should have done to start with. She typed up a fax message of her own:

Please send more complete job description for toy maker's position. Interested party needs additional details, salary range.

Yanking the paper out of the printer, she marched to the newsroom fax machine and punched out the number printed on the top of the hoax fax. And when the fax went through, the little window that normally revealed either the receiving telephone number or company name read, "K. Kringle, toy maker."

"Oh, give me a break," Virginia muttered as she waited for her short message to transmit. "The whole world is off its noodle."

And she went back to her desk, determined to approach this story with the proper touch of humor and sentimentality that would satisfy Ozzie's schmaltzy streak. But before she could close out the memo she'd just printed, she heard the fax machine whirring into action. Feeling a vague anxiety, she walked slowly toward the machine. She tore the paper off the machine:

Please excuse us, but things are so hectic this time of year. Applicants must apply in person. Just hang a left at the tundra line.

"Everybody's a comedian," she grumbled, stalk-ing over to Ozzie's desk and flinging the message under his nose.

"This is the dumbest story you've ever asked me for, Ozzie. Tops. Bar none. You win."

"Aw, lighten up, Virginia. Where's your Christmas spirit?"

"I left it in my other coat, okay? You don't really want me to write this, do you?"

Then she told him about the Santa with the real beard and the operators who seemed to be in on this dumb hoax and the name in the window on the fax machine. And when she finished, Ozzie said something that was more bizarre than everything else she'd heard today.

"Thank goodness we've still got some money in the travel budget."

"What are you talking about, Ozzie?"

"I don't see where we have a choice, Holley. You're going to have to chase this one."

Virginia's mouth went dry. She didn't like the way this was shaping up. At all. "What are you talking about, Ozzie?"

"You'll have to go up there."

"Up where?"

"The North Pole."

That was when Virginia decided she might possibly be the last sane person on Earth.

Chapter Three

His droll little mouth...

Ozzie didn't have a clue that he had lost his grip on reality. Virginia gradually realized it was that simple. For almost an hour, she tried to convince him that a trek to the North Pole in search of a retiring Santa Claus ranked right up there with launching an investigation of the tooth fairy.

When he looked at her as if that idea also had merit, Virginia knew she might as well wave the white flag. She would be spending most of December slogging through snow and slipping on ice because she couldn't convince her city editor that Santa's lair at the North Pole didn't exist.

Clearly, she thought as she walked back to her desk, the competition had hatched this whole scheme in order to flush the *Chronicle*'s credibility right down the toilet.

"Which is fine, except you're the one who's stuck with a vacation in winter wonderland," she muttered, opening her Yellow Pages to the section on travel agents.

Thirty minutes later, she had discovered that—who would have guessed it?—none of the travel agents in town offered December excursions to the freezing tundra.

Where the sun never rises during the winter, Virginia reminded herself.

Each of her friendly hometown travel agents, however, recommended very matter-of-factly that she engage a private guide.

"And do you know of someone who specializes in frostbite?" she had asked each and every one of them.

Each and every one of them had assured her that most of the private guides they knew had plans to head south of the equator for the forseeable future.

"So who the heck do I get to lead me on this wild-reindeer chase?" she said aloud to the newsroom, which was empty except for the photo-lab technician, who was pitching stacks of photos onto desks.

"Where are you going, Holley?" the gangly youth asked as he handed her a stack of prints.

"In search of Santa. Where else? Assuming I can find someone crazy enough to lead a dogsled expedition to the North Pole," she said as she picked up the top photo in the stack. "Know anybody I could trust my life to in the wilds of the Arctic?"

It seemed nothing short of prophetic that she looked down into the rugged, black-and-white, eight-by-ten glossy face of Nick Closthaler.

NICK WATCHED her scrambling up the steep path and was uncertain for a moment whether or not he was in the middle of another one of his dreams.

The yarn ball on the tip of her fuzzy white cap bobbed up and down, as did her chin-length, sunshine yellow hair. She looked tiny, almost fragile, a sense that didn't diminish even as she grew closer, even as he watched her negotiate the difficult path with agility and strength.

And just as he had in all his dreams, Nick found himself wanting her. In the way he wanted fresh air and a long swallow from a clear mountain stream, he wanted her. Almost as if another survival instinct had sprung up to join the ones he had been born with.

But he wasn't about to let this turn out the way his dreams had. He had his head on straight, and he knew the difference between fantasy and reality.

Didn't he?

Then she topped the ridge. Her baby blue eyes stared right into his. The edges of reality blurred.

"I'm back," she said brightly, a sunny smile on her face, which was rosy with cold air and exertion. Nick wondered if her cheeks were cool and silky from the mountain air, or warm velvet from the exertion of her climb.

"Yes."

No other response seemed necessary—or even safe—to Nick as he extended a hand and hoisted her over the ledge. Her hands were gloved. He felt only the strength of good leather, but longed for smooth flesh.

He reminded himself once again, as she straightened her jacket and peered across the valley, that she didn't belong in his world. No matter what his dreams said, no matter what this incessant voice in his head said, this Virginia Holley had no place with Nick Closthaler.

"How can you bear to leave it?" she asked, her voice soft with wonder as she took in his view.

"What?" He felt thickheaded around her, as if everything were coming to him through a curtain of snowflakes.

"When you go off on your adventures. How can you bear to leave this view? It's so beautiful here."

"It's beautiful everywhere."

"Is it?"

She turned her innocent, wonder-filled eyes to his, and in them he could see anew the splendor of the Nile and the mystery of the Congo and the unfailing majesty of the Himalayas. He felt an unmistakable urge to show this woman those things, which had for years been his greatest love; in her eyes, he felt, they would once again be new.

"Is your face warm?"

She looked as surprised at hearing his question as he felt in asking it. With a confused frown, she reached up to touch her face with her gloved hand.

"Are we having the same conversation?" she asked with a small laugh.

"I just . . . wondered. About your skin." And without considering the impropriety of his action, he brushed his knuckles across one round cheek. The skin was cool and silken and it burned through him in an instant.

He dropped his hand. She stepped back. She was still staring at him with wonder in her eyes. This time, Nick knew, the wonder was not for the Colorado scenery but for that lick of fire when their flesh met.

"You've come for me."

She nodded, the mesmerized nod of one who is still uncertain of her surroundings. "I need your help."

"With what?" As if it mattered. Nick knew he would go, no matter what it was. This soft, pale woman with the will to climb this mountain for him not once, but twice, somehow had the power to lure him anywhere.

She laughed and looked down at her toes. When she looked up again, he saw that the haze of magic between them had disappeared. But only for the moment; he understood that. He could bring it back anytime. With a word. A touch.

"I have to find Santa Claus."

The words stung his pride. Was she making fun of him? Trying to pull something on him? Still after that damned story of hers? And was he so horny from months on this mountain that he was vulnerable to the scent of lemon soap and the sight of perfect pink lips?

"You need me for that? He's in every mall in every town in America." He wheeled to go.

She put out her hand to stop him; her gloved fingers barely spanned the outside of his sweater-clad biceps. Power surged through him.

"No, I mean the real Santa. The one... the one at the North Pole. And you're the only one... that is, you've done that kind of thing before. You could take me there. Couldn't you?"

In her face, he saw no deception, no irony, no coyness. She was serious. But he knew that from something more than the look in her eyes. He knew it from the visions that had been haunting his days and nights these past weeks.

This was what had been calling him.

Damned if he would answer.

"Lady—" he turned and took her by the shoulders "—do you know what it's like up there this time of year?"

"It's cold. I know that. But..."

"Cold? Lady, it goes beyond cold to something else entirely." It wasn't the cold part that frightened him; it was the part about Santa Claus. The part about chasing down a myth. Frightened him because it sounded completely and plausibly rational. Now *that* was scary. So he focused on the weather, the part he understood, the part he knew he could handle. "Do you know how thirty below feels? It makes a Colorado winter feel like August in Death Valley."

"I know, but—"

"No, you don't know." He was snapping at her, not so much because of her wide-eyed insistence that she could handle an Arctic winter, but because he was on the verge of saying yes. "You can lose a toe or a finger or a cute little turned-up nose to frostbite in the time it takes you to change gloves. It's dark all the time. Twenty-four hours a day. No sunshine. Ever."

"But when there's a full moon—I checked and next week is the full moon, you know—all that moonlight on the snow, it's almost like daylight. Isn't it?"

He knew what it was like. That eerie, silver-blue haze illuminating the landscape. He could see her in that light, her pale eyes darkened, her hair glowing like spun silver, her skin pale and translucent.

"No!" He realized when she flinched that he had answered more vehemently than he had intended. He loosened his grip on her shoulders and softened the belligerence in his voice. "No. I'd have to be crazy to go up there now. Especially..."

"Especially what?" Her chin raised, and he saw the suspicious light in her eyes. It turned to a challenge when he didn't answer. "Especially what? Especially with a woman? Is that it, Nick?"

"Look..."

The heel of her palm shoved against his chest, and he staggered slightly, surprised and somehow pleased with the strength in her small frame.

"Don't you ever do that, Nick Closthaler. Ever. Don't patronize me because I'm a woman. Do you hear me?"

Nick smothered the urge to smile because he knew she would misinterpret it. But her anger, the forcefulness with which she confronted him, pleased him. Enormously. He wondered if she would flinch if a sleek, black water moccasin dropped down out of the jungle into the bow of her boat. She would, of course—only a fool wouldn't—but he suspected her recovery would be quick and her action decisive.

When you spent time in the few remaining uncivilized territories on earth, you learned to spot instantly who would help you and who would hinder you. Nick's verdict was that Virginia Holley would never hinder.

Unless I let her cloud my judgment, Nick reminded himself.

"I hear you. But I still won't take you to the Arctic Circle at this time of year. Next summer, maybe. I'll talk to you about it next summer."

"Next summer will be too late. I have to go now. And we'll pay you well. Whatever your going rate is, the paper is prepared to pay."

"No. I'm telling you, it's just not possible."

She merely stared at him, a diamond-bright hardness forming in those pale blue eyes of hers. Nick didn't believe he'd ever seen a pair of eyes that could change so quickly, could announce so many different kinds of emotions so rapidly. Or so powerfully.

"Be reasonable, Virginia, it's..."

She broke into a smile that stopped him cold. A dimpled, delighted smile. "You remembered my name."

His impatience vanished. "Of course I remembered your name. Doesn't everyone?"

"Well . . . sometimes."

Once again her eyes completely gave her away. At the moment, they reflected a long-standing hurt, and Nick wondered why it should be so special that someone remembered her name.

"Listen, Nick, I'll do whatever you want. I'll write you up as the Indiana Jones of the Arctic. I'll immortalize you in photos. I'll go away after and never breathe your name again. Whatever you want. Just take me."

"Why?"

She stared at him blankly. "Why?"

He nodded. "Why?"

She pursed her lips tightly and narrowed her eyes. "Because I have a job to do. Okay? And I always do my job. I always get the story."

"Why?"

She clapped her hands against her thighs and glared up at him. "Asking the questions is my job, Nick. Got it?"

"Why?"

"Because . . ."

She turned away. Nick saw her back stiffen as she stared out over the valley. When she spoke, her voice teetered on the edge of control. "Because it's the only thing anybody's ever needed me for. This job, I mean. Getting the story. It's all I . . . have to offer."

He didn't say anything, giving her the chance to compose herself, wishing he hadn't pushed her for an answer she shouldn't have had to give. He only knew that he needed to understand her, needed to get some idea where Virginia Holley really fit in this crazy scheme he was so tempted to let her suck him into.

She whirled to face him, her eyes now hard with defiance. "Satisfied?"

He had seen that defiance before. In his dream. In that dream he had seen swirling snow, howling wind and a woman he swore was Virginia, with just that determined look on her face.

Nick had never run away from anything in his life, except perhaps his father's way of life—and his father's ghost. And he didn't want to start now. But the idea of helping this explosive little woman track down a fat man in a red suit made him feel as if he had hit upon quicksand, despite the Arctic setting of her proposition.

Even a man who didn't run away from things knew better than to advance in the face of quicksand.

"Find yourself another sucker," he said abruptly. "Kids are depending on me this time of year. I don't have time for your crazy scheme."

He turned and stalked to his cabin, listening for the sound of her footsteps. He heard nothing. And when he was inside his cabin, he looked out to see her start back down the mountain.

The sight made him acutely aware of the emptiness inside him.

THEODORE FLOUNCED across the room and flopped into the wicker chair with the hibiscus-splashed cushion.

"Don't pout, Theodore." Roxanne checked the shine on her newly buffed nails. "I told you Maui is never any fun this time of year."

Theodore groaned, a shrill, pained sound that was as theatrical as he could make it. "Of all times to be stuck here on this sunny pile of volcanic ash!"

"You should have thought of that before you planned your little coup, Teddy. Exile isn't a pretty business."

Theodore didn't even look at Roxanne. He would gladly overdose her with Elfin Elixir right this minute. Without a qualm. Without one iota of regret. Because he knew Roxanne. She was enjoying every minute of his dismay.

"He's barely four hundred years old!" Theodore protested. "And a workaholic of the first order. Classic Type A. Who could have known he would decide to retire now?"

He pushed his short but rotund frame out of the nauseatingly bright Hawaiian chair and stalked to the window as forcefully as his forty-five inches allowed. Sand. Sunshine. Everywhere he looked. Not an evergreen in sight. Only those blasted palm trees.

"When I'm Santa, I won't deliver to anyone south of the Tropic of Cancer," he muttered petulantly. "I swear I won't."

"Exile has done nothing for your personality, Teddy," Roxanne drawled. "Absolutely nothing."

"Shut up, Roxanne. And don't call me Teddy."

"Besides, it isn't likely you're going to be Santa, is it, Teddy? Not anymore."

The points on Theodore's tiny ears turned a shocking shade of fuchsia. And as soon as he could breathe again, he puffed his chest out in its blue-and-yellow flowered shirt and turned in dramatic slow motion to face Roxanne.

"You know better than that, Roxanne. You wouldn't be here if you didn't know better than that."

VIRGINIA KNEW she was likely to stumble on the rocky path if she didn't slow down. But she was too angry to listen to her good sense. She dashed down the side of the mountain, trying to keep up with the plans racing through her mind.

She had been right to start with. Nick Closthaler was one of those men you just had to hate. The strong, silent type who *knew* they were right about everything.

Which left her in a real pickle. If he was too chicken to take her to the North Pole, where in the heck was she going to find someone willing to do it?

And if he wouldn't do one, simple little thing for her—such as lead her through an Arctic winter on a totally absurd quest—then what right did he have to affect her the way he did?

So angry was she, so preoccupied with her dilemma and the unwelcome physical sensations still whisking through her body, that she didn't hear the first little rumbles. Or even the subsequent rumbles, the louder ones, the more insistent ones. By the time her ears perked up and she looked around, an unrelenting squadron of rocks was rolling, tumbling, advancing rapidly in her direction.

Letting out a little squeak of fear, Virginia instantaneously calculated her chances of jumping out of the way without instigating a precipitous descent from the mountain path. Slim, said her pounding heart. Very slim, concurred the blood roaring in her ears.

But better, perhaps, than trying to hold her own against the fast-approaching boulders.

In her instant of hesitation, Virginia felt herself lifted into the air, flying, suddenly weightless as a windblown feather. And in the exact moment that the boulders thundered over the path she had occupied, she landed with a bone-wrenching thud on a solid but comfortable bulk to the right of the path.

Catching her breath and clinging to the solid form that clutched her, Virginia looked up into a pair of silver-gray eyes. The concern in Nick's eyes spilled over into his voice.

"Are you all right?"

She peered over her shoulder and realized Nick's grasp on a clump of bush was all that stood between them and that precipitous descent she had been worried about. Somehow she knew that was all the safety net she needed.

She nodded and smiled. "Thank you."

He settled them more securely into the brush on the side of the mountain without loosening the grip that held her against the solid expanse of his chest. Now both his arms were securely around her, protective and strong. His heart thudded forcefully beneath her gloved hand. His thighs, she realized, were like solid rock beside her own trembling legs.

She'd had a close call, after all.

"Are you deaf?" he asked.

It was hard to bristle, Virginia discovered, when you are chest-to-chest and thigh-to-thigh with a man who had possibly saved your life. Actually this rescue business was a fairly pleasing experience. Strong arms. Broad chest. A hint of warm breath fluttering the hair on her forehead.

But she *was* having trouble breathing. Perhaps a cracked rib? She stirred but felt no pain. Only that weakness in her limbs, remaining, no doubt, from her fright. "I think you can let me go now."

He didn't, however. "Didn't you hear the rumble?"

Shrugging was not quite possible. Again she shifted slightly to remind him to release her. "I did not. I appreciate the rescue. Now, if you'll excuse me...?"

Still he didn't release her. She looked up, her forehead wrinkled in a deepening frown. But when her eyes met his, her forehead smoothed and her impatient twisting in his arms stilled. His expression was no longer one of concern. No longer irritation. It was pure and simple hunger.

Her heart, which had barely begun to slow, stepped up its pace once again.

"You came after me," she said, softly.

"I…" He seemed to struggle with an explanation. His face lowered almost immeasurable inches.

"Did you change your mind?" She lifted her chin, although it wasn't really necessary for their conversation.

"No, I…" She felt his breath on her cheek now. On her lips. "I just knew…"

She never did discover exactly what it was that he knew. Because their next breath drew them closer, brought their lips together gently, like the touch of a single snowflake. Every ounce of strength in Virginia's limbs disappeared as his soft, warm lips coaxed hers along. The unfamiliar sensations he triggered seeped slowly down, deeper, arousing an urgent and delicious discomfort in the most surprising places.

He released her. Too quickly, she thought, and she staggered unsteadily for a moment before she regained her equilibrium.

"When?" he asked.

"When?" This was all too hard for her to follow.

"When do we leave?"

Never. "Leave?"

"For the North Pole. We have a lot of preparation. So how soon do we leave?"

Chapter Four

The moon on the
breast of the new-fallen snow . . .

"Do you know how much this junk weighs?" Virginia grumbled.

Attuned to every sound and movement in the taiga, the Arctic forest, Nick sensed the woman behind him once again shifting her backpack as they approached the stand of evergreens.

"You're the one who insisted on dragging that ten-pound contraption with us," Nick muttered without looking back.

He felt her glaring at his back, as he had felt every mood and emotion from her in the six days since he had agreed to this insane expedition.

"Without my laptop computer, there wouldn't be much point in making the trip," Virginia retorted. "And it weighs only six point two pounds."

Nick shook his head, but couldn't help smiling.

They had started out, six days ago in Colorado, shyly hesitant about the power of their fleeting kiss.

Nick had caught himself, time and again, reliving the moment. He'd had to get tough with himself. No more kissing! An expedition was not the time, not the place, for man-woman foolishness.

If only she would quit doing all those damnable little things that did nothing but make her more appealing in his eyes. Before leaving for the Arctic, they had together gone about the business of arranging for distribution of his toys. After they finished deliveries to the families of all his children, she had looked up at him, all wide-eyed wonder, and said, "Why, this is fun, isn't it? Are you sure that's all? Isn't there more we can do?"

Her words, her eyes, had trembled in his soul, making it damned hard not to grasp her shoulders in his gloved hands, pull her to him and kiss that innocence right off her face.

But she didn't want that. And neither did he, he kept reminding himself. Not really.

Yet when their eyes caught, when their shoulders accidentally met, when nearness mingled the heat of their bodies, Nick saw in her eyes the same smoldering sensations he felt in his loins. As well as the same emotional wariness.

So instead of taking the next tentative steps another couple might take following a first kiss, Nick had chosen to bicker. Virginia seemed happy with the decision.

Their impending trek gave them plenty to bicker over.

Virginia had complained about the food. "There is not one candy bar in the whole pack. I know for a fact that candy bars provide instant energy. Am I right? Wouldn't a six-pack of Snickers be prudent here?"

Nick had complained when she brought out two packed bags— "You won't need to dress for dinner, you know. One change of clothes. That's it." —then proceeded to unpack for her and tell her exactly what to bring.

He did rather hate leaving behind that little silk nightshirt. Thermal long johns seemed a poor substitute, but he was a practical man.

Virginia gave in on the packing and the food, but she held firm on the issue of their transportation. "We can get to Canada by train. I have the schedule right here. We do not need to fly anybody's friendly skies."

"That's crazy," Nick had argued, feeling his exasperation begin to rise. "Do you realize how much longer that will take?"

She had squared her shoulders and glared at him with stubborn determination. "I hired you. That makes me the boss, right?"

"Technically." He turned and walked away, knowing her well enough by now to know that a mere five-second beat would follow before she was on his heels with a protest. He counted his steps.

Right on five, she grabbed his arm. "Technically, my foot!"

"And only until we get to the Arctic."

He knew then, even without the half hour of impolite discussion that followed, that the issue of control would be one to struggle with the rest of the trip. If it had been anyone but Virginia, anything but this crazy scheme, he would have called the whole thing off right then and there.

But he hadn't. And upon leaving Goose Bay, Canada, after another four hours of bickering over the selection and packing of supplies needed for this leg of the journey, Virginia had complained that his vinyl pack was twice the size of the one he packed for her.

He ignored her now, as he had then.

She was, as he had known she would be, trouble. She questioned everything he did, always wanted to know why, and was never satisfied to simply take an order.

He liked that about her. And that, he knew, made him as crazy as he had already decided she must be.

As he stepped beyond the last of the trees of the taiga, Nick stopped instinctively to relish the feeling of awe the tundra always inspired. When he did, he sensed Virginia behind him, sidestepping to avoid him. She stumbled, no doubt off balance from the unaccustomed weight she carried on her back. He reached for her arm to right her. She opened her mouth, the expression on her face telling him that she was ready to light into him for stopping so abruptly.

Then her eyes registered what lay before them, and her open mouth fell silent. He knew what she was seeing and how she was feeling.

Ice.

Acres of ice glittered in the light of a full moon that seemed to occupy half the dark purple sky. One relentless sheet of ice stretched before them all the way to the horizon, which blurred into eerie, half-lit darkness. The effect was broken only by an occasional jut of glacial mountain, rising into the sky like the broken shards of an oversize ice sculpture.

She gasped.

"Welcome to the tundra." He spoke softly, hoping his voice would calm the emotions he saw spilling in rapid waves over her face.

Virginia nodded. Her eyes were still stunned, but he could see the tide of panic rising there.

"We're... that is... how far? To the... Pole?"

Nick shrugged out of his pack, settling it onto the ice with a sharp crack. "I don't know exactly. A hundred miles? Two?"

Her pale face grew suddenly paler in the silvery haze of the moonlight.

He felt her control slipping, falling prey to the terror she was giving off in rays. Even as he wondered if anyone but him would pick up the emotional signals she broadcast, he tried to transmit his own signals. Confidence. Control. Courage.

After a moment of uncertainty, she seemed to receive them; he could tell from the slight lift of her chin. But for a few instants at least, the magnitude of the tundra was too powerful to overcome. She was still afraid; he remembered that fear. He had felt it, too, the first time.

She had flinched, as he had always known any sane person would. Now was the time to see if he had judged her rightly.

"It's not too late," he said, again softly. He understood; if she backed down, who could blame her?

"What?" Her response had a dazed quality.

"We can still turn back."

The offer seemed to calm her. He watched her straighten her spine. She pulled the fur-lined hood of her down parka tighter around her face, then turned that face to him.

"We're not turning back."

He studied her, mesmerized by the courage in her face, a courage that was stronger than her fear. Not many women had that kind of courage. Neither did many men, for that matter. He nodded and squatted beside his pack to pull out the miniature radio transmitter cached away in a side pocket.

"Fine. We'll camp here tonight."

"Is it night?"

He smiled at the wry bewilderment in her voice. She squatted beside him, dropping her pack behind her, and watched as he readied the radio for transmission.

"Two hundred miles, huh? And we're going to... It'll be Lincoln's birthday before we can walk that far."

He keyed in the transmission code he had memorized. "Don't worry. We're not going to walk all of it.

I'm radioing now for a helicopter. It'll be here in the morning with more supplies. It'll take us deeper into the tundra and..."

"By helicopter?"

"Mm-hmm. We're lucky so far. If the humidity rises another few degrees or the wind kicks up at all, a chopper won't make it."

She stood abruptly.

"You can forget that," she said, all bewilderment now gone from her voice.

"What are you talking about?"

"I'm not going anywhere in a helicopter."

Heaving a sigh that was the closest he usually came to impatience, Nick clicked off the radio, shoved it into his parka pocket and stood. At five feet ten, it was nice to tower over someone. It would be even nicer if it gave him even the most remote sense of being in control of Virginia Holley.

"If you don't intend to go by helicopter, would you mind telling me exactly how you do plan to cover that terrain in this lifetime?"

He swept his arm in the direction of the tundra, but her eyes refused to follow his gesture. She pinned him with a penetrating gaze.

"You're the guide. You tell me."

"Exactly. I'm the guide. We're going by helicopter."

"Guess again, Closthaler. I will go by dogsled. I will walk. I will ride a reindeer if you can hail me one. But I will not go up in a helicopter!"

With that, she whirled and stalked back into the taiga, leaving him standing beside their packs to contemplate the runaway terror her eyes had revealed in the instant before she fled.

Worried she would stalk off and lose her way, Nick followed her into the forest. Before he had gone twenty yards, he saw her, huddled on the ground with her knees to her chin, leaning against one of the pines. Understanding the need to be alone with one's fears, Nick turned soundlessly and returned to set up camp for the night.

The small tent went up effortlessly. The food—sticks of hard salami for energy and fruit leather to ward off scurvy—required no preparation. In five minutes, their camp at the edge of the taiga was ready. And still Virginia had not returned. He considered going after her. But he knew he wouldn't want anyone coming after him. He owed her the same respect.

Disgruntled nonetheless, he sat leaning against his pack. He gnawed at the fruit leather, staring up at the moon-bright sky. Few stars were visible, the light of the moon so dominated the sky. He felt a measure of peace, a calmness of spirit.

But it didn't last long. He was growing increasingly impatient with her absence. In fact, he was on the verge of going after her and insisting she return to camp for the night when he heard her stomping across the ice-crusted snow on the forest floor.

She said nothing, merely sat a good four feet away from him and reached for the stick of salami. He was glad for the sight of her. She didn't eat the salami the way a man would have, tearing off bites with her teeth. Clumsy as she was in her gloves, she pulled the pocket knife from her belt and carved away dainty slices of the spicy meat. Her teeth were even and white. She licked her full, pink lips, and he tasted them with her.

"So, Closthaler, what do we do now?" she asked as she wiped the blade of her knife with snow and stashed it back in her belt.

"We call for a chopper in the morning. Or head back to Goose Bay."

She glared at him. "I don't think so."

Her cheeks glowed with the same inner fire that lit her eyes. The heat transferred itself to Nick. He squirmed in his heavy layers of clothes, uncomfortably aware of the way every inch of his skin prickled, itched with an inner need he couldn't allow himself to entertain. "You didn't do much thinking while you were pouting, did you?"

"I do not pout."

He shrugged. He was peeved that she stayed four feet away. He glanced at the tent. "Do you intend to keep me at arm's length all night?"

Her eyes flickered only briefly over the tiny tent. The color in her cheeks deepened; so did the tingling beneath the surface of his skin. "What's wrong with a dogsled?"

"Did you reserve one with Hertz before we left?"

He saw her fists clench in their insulated gloves. Definitely welterweight, but he suspected she carried quite a wallop.

"I won't fly."

"You'll have to fly." He wondered if another kiss would make her more pliant, but he doubted it.

"You'll have to think of something else."

"You'll fly or I'm on my way back to Goose Bay by morning."

She snorted derisively. "We won't see morning for another six months, Closthaler."

He gave in to the smile he felt simmering within; it deepened when she returned it. "Okay, Holley, why are you afraid of flying?"

That silenced her. The point of her chin edged up a notch and, for the moment, her pride was stronger than her anger.

"I'm going to bed," she announced haughtily. He watched her well-bundled figure climb through the narrow opening of the tent and disappear inside. Rear end last.

It was a fetching rear end, even swaddled in enough goose down to choke a polar bear.

But at least he had his answer. She *was* afraid of flying.

He wanted to follow that tempting backside, but he forced himself to take the time to cool off. Virginia needed cooling off, too, he told himself, although he doubted the source of her heat was the same as his. With deliberate slowness, he put away the food, took a final lingering look at the frosty terrain and crawled into the tent. She faced south, her back rigidly demarcating the tent squarely in the middle. He lay down beside her, feeling the warmth of her along his arm.

"You might as well tell me." He grew hard, feeling her nearness, but kept his voice soft.

She didn't reply.

"We're all afraid of something or another, you know?"

She didn't reply, but he felt the sudden rise in her body tension that said he had captured her attention.

"Want me to go first?"

She stirred, turning slightly toward him in the darkness. "Okay."

Nick frowned. What the hell was he doing admitting this? Especially to this mule-headed woman, when he'd never before admitted it to anyone else in all his thirty-two years.

"Mice."

At least the subject eased the pressure building in his recalcitrant body.

She snickered. "Nice try, Closthaler. Now, what are you *really* afraid of."

"Little white ones especially. With pink eyes. I break out in a cold sweat every time I see them at the pet store."

She rolled over. "No lie?"

"And one time—" She was closer now. Close enough to kiss. To hell with this mouse business. His confession could wait.

"Go on."

She was right. Kisses and soft breasts against his chest and the smell of woman in his nostrils, *that* would have to wait. He drew a deep breath and ignored the stirring in his body.

"One time I had a family of mice living in my workshop back home." He remembered the little gray critters and the absolute terror that had struck when one of them poked its bewhiskered nose over the edge of his workbench. He shuddered. "I couldn't bring in an exterminator—I mean, that would hardly be fair. It wasn't their fault I'm chicken."

"You? Chicken?"

He was pleased to note the skepticism in her voice. But she wasn't viewing this from where he was. Just the memory of lying in bed at night and wondering if one of the little gray critters had made its way across his yard and into his cabin gave him heart palpitations.

"So I called the science teacher at the elementary school. Her class came up and caught them for a project."

"What else?"

"What else what?"

"What else are you afraid of? Spiders?"

"Don't be ridiculous." He heard the teasing note in her voice and was at once grateful for it and embarrassed by it.

"Bumblebees?"

He hesitated. He tried reminding himself she was a reporter. But it made no difference, not any longer. He'd been hiding for a decade, and within the past week he had suddenly lost his passion for hiding. "Water."

She wriggled around in the tent, brushing against his side. "Oh, right. Mr. Macho Adventurer is afraid to get his toes wet. Tell me another one, Closthaler."

He almost groaned at her nearness. "No. I'm serious."

"Water. Like the Amazon River. The one you canoed down a year ago last summer."

This reporter had done her homework; that much was clear. "Yeah. And like the river that ran through my father's logging camp, where two men drowned the summer I was nine."

"Oh." She paused. "Then how can you do it? All your expeditions, I mean?"

"Grit my teeth. And hope I don't fall in."

"What if you did?"

"I'd probably panic myself to death before I ever managed to swallow enough water to drown."

Then he told her about the time he had slipped in a stream in Java and was having heart palpitations before he realized the water was shallow enough to stand in. He made her laugh with the tale; she was almost snuggled against him by the time he finished. "Now it's your turn."

She lapsed once again into silence, and he felt her stiffen and move to turn away. As agonizing as her nearness was, Nick couldn't face losing it. Before she could reposition herself, he counterattacked by sweeping his arm around her shoulder and holding her tightly to his side.

"Nick—" she started to protest.

"Body heat," he explained. "We need the body heat."

"We didn't need body heat last night. Or the night before."

"That was in the taiga. This is on the tundra. It's different."

"Is it?"

He didn't mind a bit that she sounded skeptical, as long as she stayed nestled in the crook of his arm.

"Now, why are you afraid of flying?"

"You didn't tell me why you're afraid of mice."

"Are you always this difficult, or do I bring out something special in you?"

She giggled again. The sound purred pleasantly against his chest.

"Remember, I'm the reporter here. I get to ask the questions. So, why are you afraid of mice."

"I don't remember."

"You don't remember?"

"I just always have been. Must've been from something when I was a kid."

"Oh."

The forlornness in her voice tipped him off.

"Is that why you're afraid of flying? Something happened when you were a kid?"

She went very still; he felt her pulling into herself emotionally.

"That's how... that's how my parents... died."

It was the voice of a lonely little girl. He pulled her closer; her head burrowed into the curve of his neck and shoulder. Her hair was soft against his cheek.

"How long ago?"

"I was five."

Nick closed his eyes against the sudden anguish in his heart. Nothing pained him more than seeing children hurt; right now he couldn't see the hurt, but he could hear the hurt child in her voice. His heart broke.

"Of course, I don't remember them very well. Not anymore. I remember my father singing me to sleep most nights. And my mother baking gingerbread men every Christmas. But mostly... I don't really remember what they looked like, except..."

He heard the catch in her voice and squeezed her again.

"Except for the pictures in the locket. My mother had a locket with their pictures in it. I loved that locket. I would lie on her bed while she was dressing to go out, just looking at the gold locket."

"Do you still have the locket?"

"No. It was... lost. Maybe she was wearing it. I don't know."

"I'm sorry, Virginia."

She put a hand on his chest. "I like it when you say my name."

"Go to sleep now, Virginia."

He felt her relax.

"Nick? About tomorrow..."

"Don't worry about tomorrow. I know where we can get a great deal on a dogsled expedition."

"You do?"

"I'm the guide, aren't I?"

They were both silent for a long time. Finally, when his heart was not quite so full with visions of an abandoned little girl named Virginia, he heard her breathing grow steady.

Only then did he let himself fall asleep.

ELSA SHOOK her head in dismay as she viewed the sleeping couple through the grainy screen of the old-fashioned Vista Master.

"Maybe Noel's right," Kris muttered, squinting through his bifocals at the fuzzy image on the flat, square screen.

"About what?" Elsa asked, still preoccupied with how distressingly incompatible this young couple from Colorado had appeared for the past few days. Even so, it seemed highly inappropriate to her that they should be lying there, side by side, in such a small tent with no chaperon and—

"About that newfangled computerized World-View," Kris interjected. "It does have color. And surround-sound. Got to stay current, you know."

Elsa sniffed and patted the cumbersome pewter box that housed the naughty-and-nice surveillance system Noel had created. "Vista Master has been fine for more than two hundred years. It will be fine for a long time to come."

Kris shrugged and pulled the screen down over the image. "Be that as it may, I suspect our young couple there will have plenty of newfangled ideas once they take over."

Her husband's words made Elsa feel a trifle queasy. She watched him settle into his overstuffed chair by the hearth and prop his booted feet on the fur-covered hassock. Hands folded over his tummy, he closed his eyes and basked in the warmth of the crackling fire. The morning's bag of mail, postmarked from around the world, patiently awaited attention at his side.

Frowning and shaking her head, Elsa followed him and perched on the edge of her chair, which was downscaled for her shorter frame. The chairs were covered in pleasantly worn tapestry, in soft colors of moss green and peach, unlike anything else in the brightly colored, anything-but-elegant Toyland Compound. A wizened toy maker in Austria had made them more than four hundred years ago, when they were just starting out in this business. She would miss the chairs and suspected Kris would, too.

"Kris, before you get too comfortable, I think we need to discuss something," she said, keeping her voice very businesslike and hoping he would respond in kind. She hated to think of it, but sometimes Kris did exhibit just the faintest streak of male chauvinism. Oh, not much, mind you. But he did so hate it when little girls wrote asking for toy trucks. He sometimes took them baby dolls, too. Just for good measure, he said.

Anyway, she hoped he would take her seriously right now.

He opened his eyes drowsily and peered over the tops of his bifocals. "Yes, my dear."

"Is it possible... that is, do you think... oh, dear. It's just that, I worry you've chosen the wrong couple for the task at hand."

Kris frowned, then struggled to a more upright position in his armchair. "How can you say that? I studied this thing extensively. I've had my eye on these two for years. They're perfect. You saw them. How can you say they aren't perfect?"

She hesitated. "Well, they don't seem to get along very well."

He waved dismissively. "Bah! You didn't see them kiss in Sugarplum Bluff, Colorado. I did."

"Yes, but..."

"Besides, haven't you ever seen a Katharine Hepburn–Spencer Tracy movie? It's the mechanics of love, my dear. Only natural they should... mmm... grate a little, at first."

"I see." She couldn't have disagreed more, Tracy and Hepburn aside. But perhaps another tactic was in order. "Be that as it may, Kris. What about this Virginia's fear of flying? Oh, my, Kris, you must admit that's quite distressing. What if flu strikes again, as it did in '25... or was that '26? I never can remember. But if this young man Nick—and that is a nice name,

I do admit—but if he comes down with fever and is as...discommoded...as you were, well, where would we be then?"

"She'll get over that."

"But how will they even get here, Kris? If she won't take the helicopter and..."

"It's taken care of." And he settled back deeper into his chair, plucked the bifocals off his nose and dropped them onto the top of the bulging mail sack. His lids eased shut again.

"But, Kris..."

Without moving, he smiled and interrupted her. "Don't fret, Elsa. When all is said and done, Nick and Virginia will be the perfect Mr. and Mrs. Claus II."

Now completely frustrated, Elsa sighed and stood to go. But when she reached the door, she turned back to leave him with one more thought before she checked on candy cane bending and wrapping.

"Kris, I cannot recall that you and I *ever* grated. Even a little."

Chapter Five

More rapid than eagles...

By the time the Akuchti village came into view on the horizon late the next afternoon, Virginia was more grateful than ever for the bottomless layers of cotton and wool and down Nick had insisted she wear. When he had first outfitted her for their journey, she had resented every additional layer, which only added another inch horizontally without modifying her vertically at all.

In other words, she felt like a blimp.

And feeling like a blimp under Nick's watchful eyes made her grouchy.

But she was warm and had been all day, as they skirted the edges of the taiga, heading west toward the Eskimo village Nick assured her was ahead. Surprisingly warm on the outside, unaccustomedly warm on the inside.

That she was able to talk about her parents the night before had surprised her. She hadn't told anyone so much about her feelings since Penny Brown announced to her they were going to be best friends that first day at her new school in the eighth grade. And she hadn't thought of her mother's locket in years; she had been astonished at her powerful longing to lay eyes on the intricate piece of gold-and-cloisonné jewelry again.

But the most surprising thing of all was that, with Nick listening and consoling her, she hadn't felt the quiver of emptiness inside that the memory of her parents usually elicited. Warm, cozy feelings had filled her from top to bottom.

Very warm, very cozy feelings.

She remembered the comfort of Nick's thick, strong arm beneath her neck and around her shoulders, his breath warm on her forehead through the night.

Just as well she looked a blimp, she told herself as she shifted the strap of her backpack. Neither one of them needed to be getting ideas.

"Thank goodness," she breathed when Nick pointed out the ice huts on the horizon and other signs of what passed for civilization in this most uncivilized climate. "I'm about to drop."

"Don't drop yet. We'll be lucky to make it by mealtime."

Although she had learned not to mistrust Nick's judgment, she gazed ahead with skepticism. "But..."

"The horizon is a long ways off up here."

Squelching the groan that rose in her throat, she kept trudging along behind Nick. His footprints swallowed the tiny impression of her boot; no wonder she felt safe with him beside her in the night.

Again she forced herself to shake off her awareness of Nick and concentrate on the other discomforts of the moment. "I'm going to kill him."

He turned to look at her without slowing. "Who?"

"Ozzie." She noted the wry twist of his lips and pretended she couldn't remember the feel of those lips moving over hers. "My boss. The madman who sent me up here in the first place."

He nodded. "I'll help, if you like."

She smiled. She was discovering a certain appeal in the strong, silent type. Especially when the silence was accompanied by straightforward gray eyes whose color changed from that of early-morning mist to the slate-darkness of a stormy sky. Right now they were soft and shimmering. She looked away. "You know what Ozzie's doing right now?"

Nick shook his head.

"I can see him right now, sprawled in front of his fireplace." She paused and sighed deeply. "Oh, I can feel the warmth right now. On my feet. And he's probably got a heavy-duty eggnog balanced on his belly—he has ample room to serve quite a holiday buffet, trust me. And he's watching *How the Grinch Stole Christmas* on TV. Probably rooting for the grinch."

She glared into the expanse of blue-white ice. "When I get back to Colorado, I'm going to tear him limb from pudgy limb."

If I get back to Colorado.

She shivered at the thought and sneaked a look at Nick. She had learned, in the three days they had traveled together, that simply looking at him gave her confidence. A glance at him, and safety was something tangible. Security wrapped itself around her and warmed her, even here in this pitiless world of ice and wind.

And sometimes, when she looked at Nick, she wondered if he would ever again kiss her. Or was that one little expedition she was going to have to launch all on her own?

THE EIGHTY-NINE AKUCHTI whose winter village lay on the edge of the tundra were prepared for their arrival.

Caribou and seal turned on spits over sheltered fires. Music greeted them. Round, ruddy faces smiled and offered welcome in both native tongue and broken English. Small children who had never seen white people were brought close for a better view.

As Virginia gnawed a piece of the tough, greasy seal meat, she wondered what would happen if this high-fat diet caused her to outgrow her new winter outfits before she completed her assignment. Sure, they'd done a good amount of walking the past four days, but that was about to come to an end.

Besides the feast and celebration awaiting them, a team of the strongest huskies had already been groomed to depart the next day. Sleds made of wood, bone and rawhide had been stocked with ample provisions. And three of the stocky young Akuchti men were prepared to accompany them and had already discussed with Nick the route they were to take.

The huge bonfire was allowed to die, and the celebratory drum music hushed to a restful purr. Seal-oil lamps glowed within many of the igloos dotting the landscape. And the fading firelight flickered softly on Nick's face; she liked the chiseled look of it, even now that several days of not shaving were catching up with him. She leaned closer, resisting the urge to touch him, and whispered, "How did you let them know we were coming?"

"I didn't."

Her reporter's skepticism surfaced. "They were certainly well prepared for something nobody had told them about."

His face grew guarded, his lips tighter with a tension she was now growing accustomed to seeing. She liked it better when they softened. He said nothing.

"Well, they certainly know *you.*"

"I've been before."

"And you expect me to believe they just prepared all this—a feast, entertainment, our supplies—on the off chance you might show up again and want to do a little sight-seeing in the dead of winter?"

"I didn't say they didn't know we were coming."

"But..."

"I said I didn't tell them."

"Oh. Right. I suppose Ozzie called their 800 number and made advance reservations."

He turned, and even in the darkness she could make out his expression. For the first time since she'd met him, he looked uncertain, almost bewildered.

"No. I suspect it was whoever, whatever, is orchestrating this whole adventure."

His words sent an uncontrollable shake through her. "What do you mean?"

He hesitated. "You don't really think we're in control here, do you?"

"Well, *I'm* certainly not. You're supposed to be. We're spending a lot of *Chronicle* money this week, and if..." Her weak protest fizzled out. That wasn't what he meant, and she knew it. "I don't want to hear this."

"I know just how you feel."

And he stared at her a long time before he stood and joined Tom Elkhorn, the Akuchti who would lead their party of five when they set out in the morning. Virginia stared after him, feeling stripped of some defense she hadn't even known she needed.

"Sun lady?"

She turned toward the voice. A little boy, rotund in his thickly layered clothing, held a younger girl by the hand. The little girl was staring at Virginia's head; the little boy's gaze flickered shyly to her face, then away.

She smiled at them and beckoned. "Yes?"

"My sister, she want touch sun in hair."

Virginia reached up; a fluff of blond bangs peeked out from beneath the hood of her jacket.

"She never see sun lady before." He grinned shyly. "Me, too."

Smiling, Virginia eased her hood back to reveal more of her hair. Both pairs of dark eyes widened in plump, nut brown faces. She leaned closer and waited for their shy, tentative touch. At the first brush against Virginia's hair, the little girl sprang back and giggled. She spoke to the little boy in Akuchti.

"She say... um... soft. Like first snow."

The children touched her hair again, and within minutes all fourteen children in the village had gathered to touch hair they judged to be the color of the summer sun and the texture of new-fallen snow. Unused to being the center of attention, Virginia knew her cheeks were red, especially when she caught sight of Nick watching from the shadows.

Stronger than her embarrassment, however, was her joy at being in the circle of children. She hugged each and every one of them and felt the possessive tug inside her as their warm bodies wriggled close to her. Even through the barrier of extra clothes, their pudgy arms and cuddly frames touched the emptiness deep inside her, giving it short-lived warmth.

Then their mothers came to round them up and ship them off to bed for the night. The spot inside Virginia grew cool once again as, one by one, they drifted away and left her staring into the darkness.

"Children like you."

Nick's voice filled some of the void she had only recognized once the children were gone.

"Do you think?" She let him pull her to her feet. The gentle pleasure she had felt with the physical contact with the children shifted to another kind of pleasure, another kind of connection, with the touch of his hand. "Someday... someday I'd like to..."

He waited for her to finish, but she couldn't quite put her finger on what longing she wished to express. When she was silent for more than a minute, he said, "Have children of your own?"

She shrugged and nodded uncertainly. The connection she felt with Nick made it easier to admit, yet harder, too. "That, too. But more than that. Something... I don't know... bigger than that."

"Something that will touch lots of children."

He didn't ask. The certainty with which he spoke reminded her of his work in Sugarplum Bluff. "Yeah. Something to make it up to all the kids who grew up... the way I did. Or worse. Something like you do."

He smiled, then shook his head. "No. Bigger than that, I think."

And she felt somehow that he was right. She felt something more, too, as he took her hand and led her to the ice hutch they had been given for the night. It was as if he had somehow made a silent commitment to join her as she set out to do this thing she couldn't even identify.

They crawled through the entrance tunnel, dug lower than the floor to block out blowing wind, then up into the main room. When they snuffed out the seal-oil lamp and lay down in the surprisingly cozy hutch, Virginia put up no pretense that she preferred lying apart. She pulled herself against Nick's strong, solid side and smiled as he put his arm around her in a now-familiar embrace.

It all felt so right. Almost preordained. And she remembered his remark from earlier in the evening.

"You think we're...that this is some kind of mission?"

His voice was cautiously thoughtful. "I think someone wants us here."

"That sounds so...ominous." She wished there were some way to put a lid on her growing awareness of him. Her skin was alive with his nearness, her breasts tight, her lips hungry, the deepest parts of her thrumming demandingly.

"I don't think it's ominous. But I think there's something at work here. Something greater than either of us."

"Destiny?"

"At first I thought it was just me."

She, too, had wondered if she were the only one feeling the way she was feeling, or was he equally aware of her? "And now?"

"I think we're in this together."

She swallowed hard. "Together?"

He murmured his assent.

Together. The idea appealed to her. But right now she felt the need for a lot more togetherness than Nick apparently had in mind. He had kissed her before, then shown no more inclination. Now she had to know if that was lack of interest or merely restraint. She had to know if the heat of that moment was merely her reaction to the danger of the rock slide, or her reaction to Nick.

Baloney! She didn't need to know. She already knew. The real truth was, she simply wanted to feel it again. Wanted the tides within her body to rise and fall once again with the impatience of his lips on hers.

She made her voice light, tried to keep all the strain of unanswered need out of it. "Then I think you should kiss me good-night. As long as it's destiny."

"I'm not sure I can do that," he replied after a moment of hesitation.

"I can show you."

She heard him chuckle.

"But what if I don't want to stop at a good-night kiss?"

She raised her head and stared up at his face, which was coming into focus as her eyes adjusted to the dark. He was smiling gently.

"You needn't think I'm going to do any unnecessary disrobing in this weather," she retorted softly even as she half hoped he would be so impassioned he would want her to do just that.

He chuckled again and she joined him.

By the time their laughter had died, they were nose to nose. His breath tickled her lips, warm and seductive. She inched her face forward the minuscule distance necessary to bring their lips together.

His mouth accepted hers tenderly, beginning a lazy exploration that definitely spoke little of good-nights. His lips urged. His fingertips caressed. She felt tiny in his embrace, fragile and sheltered. And when she quivered with a need for something more, he at last pressed to her more urgently. He pulled her body as close as their clothing would allow, anchoring her head with one large hand. Her breasts ached against his chest, her thighs grew warm with the need to pull him to her, into her. His mouth pressed against hers, and she opened to the welcome invasion.

His restraint had vanished remarkably quickly; so had hers.

She was breathing so raggedly she barely heard the moan from deep in his chest, was barely aware when he gradually tapered off the intensity of the kiss.

"Sleep now," he whispered.

She wished he hadn't been so adamant about unnecessary disrobing.

But she slept as peacefully as a child tucked safely and lovingly into bed.

"ARE YOU AFRAID?" Virginia asked when Nick stepped into place behind one of the sleds that would speed their journey the next morning.

He saw in her round blue eyes that she was.

"No."

Her uneasiness transformed itself quickly to cynicism.

"Not real fear," he conceded. Not the heart-tripping, teeth-rattling fear he had seen in others. "That kind of fear is deadly."

"Deadly?" She looked out over the terrain they would set out to conquer in a matter of moments.

He took her by the shoulders and turned her to face him. "Deadly. It robs you of your judgment and slows your reactions. I don't have that luxury. And neither do you."

Her chin stiffened defiantly. "Anybody would be crazy not to be afraid of this. Don't pull that macho act on me, Closthaler."

"That's not fear," he said. "That's healthy respect for an opponent. That's adrenaline. Racehorse nerves. It gives you an edge. But it's not fear."

He watched the play of thoughts and emotions in her eyes as she took in his words. Their blue depths moved from the edge of panic to wary comprehension.

"We *could* die." She said the words matter-of-factly.

"Plenty have."

She nodded.

"It's still not too late," he reminded her gently.

The wariness in her eyes hardened to resolve. "How often do you back down, Nick?"

"Only when it's necessary."

"Will we know when it's necessary?"

"We'll know."

The resolve in her expression wavered only momentarily. Then she looked up at him with that wry expression he was beginning to anticipate.

"Ozzie's going to owe me big for this one." Drawing a deep breath, she looked over the sleds. "Now, which one do I drive?"

"You *ride* in this one," he said, pointing to the narrow space he had left for her amid the supplies in his sled.

"Ride? I'm not going to *ride*. I'm going to pull my own weight on this trip."

"Ah. You're experienced at this? I had no idea."

"Well, no, but—"

"Then you ride."

"I'm telling you—"

"No, *I'm* telling *you*. These things zip over slick ice. Almost two hundred pounds of supplies is balanced on each one. And four animals are depending on the guide for directions. This is not a lark, Virginia. This is where the healthy respect comes in. Now, climb in the sled."

She held her ground, but he saw the stubbornness die out of her face. "You could teach me."

"How much do you weigh?"

Her face pinched up tightly. "One hundred. And ... ten."

"In all those clothes, maybe. Virginia, each one of those dogs weighs more than half what you weigh. Men and women may be equal, but until you weigh in at one-sixty-five or so, you don't have what it takes to manage a sled team."

She looked ready to protest, but eventually she acknowledged his logic with a nod. "Okay. Then what do I do?"

He respected her, both for giving in to reason and for her stubborn refusal to be deadweight on the trip. "Come on. I'll introduce you to the dogs. You can care for them."

Although she did express some skepticism that feeding and watering the dogs was not a big enough job compared to piloting one of the teams, Nick soon convinced her otherwise. Keeping them well fed was time-consuming. Keeping them hydrated, when anything liquid wanted nothing more than to harden into ice, was no small job.

"By the end of the day, you'll know these mutts intimately," Nick promised. "But don't forget, they're not pets. They're just a hair away from the wild."

He watched as she looked into the canny eyes of a big gray husky, which stared back with a look both soulful and riveting.

"Okay," she told the animal, its tail curved high over its back to prevent freezing. "You may be the boss, but we're on the same team. Got it?"

The animal twitched an ear, studying her unwaveringly, measuring her worth, Nick suspected. An Arctic sled dog was a good judge of character, Nick knew; he felt confident Virginia would prove herself and they would accept her.

They set out, the sled piloted by the senior Akuchti, Tom Elkhorn, in the lead, followed by Nick, then two of the younger Akuchti, Chuck and Antok, in the rear. As the bitter wind whipped into his face, drawing tears to his eyes and almost instantly numbing his stocking-covered cheeks and nose, Nick tried to block out Tom's explanation of his insistence on accompanying them.

"Need protect," Tom had said the night before, his square face and dark eyes solemn. "Cannot go alone. Must have protect."

"You can't protect me from the cold," Nick had protested.

Tom had nodded his agreement. "Is true. Other forces. Not all good. Need protect."

Then Tom had lapsed into inscrutable silence.

Chapter Six

*The prancing and pawing
of each little hoof...*

Theodore was in a snit.

He was having one heck of a time keeping his creamy white thighs from becoming that disgusting shade of golden brown everyone turned in the tropic sunshine. Commercial sunscreens reacted violently with Elfin Elixir, he had discovered to his abject mortification. A liberal slathering of the sticky mess had sent him fading in and out. One minute he might be hiding under a palm tree, plotting ways to still the noxious pounding of the surf, and the next minute all that remained of him was his floral shirt, baggy shorts and rubber thongs, propped in place without him.

Someone had suggested coconut milk. But Theodore quickly discovered that mosquitoes loved the sweet flavor of the stuff. He had not turned brown, to be sure, but he was covered with livid pink welts for days.

When Roxanne arrived, he was conniving ways to bring on a month-long typhoon while holed up inside the ridiculous thatch-roofed hut he rented by the month. Everyone staying at this overpriced resort thought the huts were so adorably *native;* they gave Theodore sinusitis.

"Anything to put an end to this sunshine!" he moaned as Roxanne materialized on his chaise longue.

"Are you piddling away your powers again?" she asked, uncurling her toes as she wriggled into a comfortable spot on the lounge.

"I may have to live here, thanks to the incompetence of those I trusted to help me execute Kris's ouster," Theodore snapped. "But I don't have to put up with interminable sunshine!"

He ignored her for as long as he could, trying to calculate the exact level of elixir-intensified alpha waves necessary to create a high-pressure system off the coast of Guam. But it became obvious that without some prodding the pouty little gremlin wasn't going to tell him why she was here.

He sat back in his chair. "Okay. What is it?"

"Oh, you mean you're interested?"

She leered at him from beneath half-closed lids. He had found her an amusing sort in the old days, before his exile.

"Spit it out, Roxie."

"They're on their way."

"Who?"

"Nick and Virginia."

"Nick and... Who the heck are Nick and Virginia?"

"The heirs apparent. They departed from the Akuchti in a party of five this morning."

"Those blasted Akuchti!"

"It's interesting, though."

"What's that?"

"The pretenders to the throne, they don't seem to know why they've been called."

Theodore's lavender eyes grew wide. "You mean nobody's told them?"

Roxanne giggled. "I'm not even sure the woman believes in Santa Claus."

Theodore snickered. Giggled. Chortled. Laughed until he howled. He laughed until he was rolling on the floor and his toes had curled up even more tightly. He laughed until the points of his ears began to flap in the tropical breeze wafting through the open sliding glass door.

Finally he managed to speak.

"This is lovely. The old fool's gone off his rocker. He's recruited two humans who don't even know what's hit 'em." Theodore sprang to his feet in one swift motion and snapped his fingers. "Okay. Here's the plan. You go back to the pole and pull all our confederates together. When the lovely couple arrive, we'll—"

"Mmm, Teddy?"

"What?"

"About our cohorts?"

He didn't like her wary tone of voice. "What about them?"

"Well, we don't exactly have any."

"What are you talking about? What about Rusty? And Sasha? And Marvin? What about Skeezix and Biddy and Glert? The grinch patrol is thirty-six strong. What are you talking about?"

Roxanne looked down at her hands, and Theodore knew he was in for another dose of extremely bad news.

"Well, everybody's...we've been abandoned, Teddy. It's just me and you."

"Knaves! Rapscallions! Twisted deviants!" He knew he was turning fuchsia and was absolutely powerless to stop himself. "Everybody?"

Roxanne nodded.

He paced. He paced for almost half an hour. He must have covered enough territory to get him halfway across Maui by the time he halted in front of Roxanne, his ears a calmer shade of mauve.

"The scoundrels will regret this. But we're not going to let it slow us down."

"But Teddy..."

"You have to decide now, Roxie. In or out?"

She looked at him dubiously. "I get to make truffles instead of gingerbread?"

"Anything. The kitchen will be your domain, Rox."

"And I won't have to give any of them away if I don't want to?"

"Roxie, we've covered this territory before. In or out? What'll it be?"

She took a deep breath. "In."

"Okay. Here's what we'll do." He tossed a notepad and pencil into her lap. "Get this down. I want you to put together a media campaign. When this thing breaks, I want us to be ready. Slogan. Logo. Definitely a new line of Santa gear. No more of this red-flannel-and-fur junk. See if you can get Alexander Julian on it. I want something flashy. Something very twenty-first century."

Roxanne scribbled rapidly. Theodore paused to rub his nose and think for a moment.

"Maybe we'll do a video. When the reindeer patties hit the fan, we'll commandeer air time on every TV station in the world."

"We will?"

"A new Santa has captured the throne!" In one elegant leap, he landed atop his desk, legs astraddle, arms extended. "A new Santa! A Santa who wants something in return! If the world wants to keep its once-a-year magic, it will pay for the privilege!"

Aware that his voice had risen to an alarmingly shrill crescendo, Theodore closed his eyes and drew a deep breath. "Power, Roxanne. I'll have all the power I'll need."

When she didn't respond, he looked down to find her nibbling the end of the pencil he had tossed her, a worried expression on her face.

"What is it, Rox?"

"If the grinch patrol has stiffed us, how're you gonna do it, Teddy? How can you take over all by yourself?"

"I have my ways." He floated to the ground on a cloud of serenity. "I can get greater forces on my side."

"Greater than Kris Kringle?"

"I have markers out. People owe me."

"Who, Teddy?"

Without answering, he snapped his fingers. "Pack my bags, Roxie. Tomorrow I'm lunching with Mother Nature."

AN ARCTIC WOLF HOWLED in the distance.

It was nothing like the friendly, tail-wagging woof of your neighbor's Lab, Virginia noted as she huddled in her tent, fighting cold, loneliness and fear of the untamed wilderness she heard in the wolf's plaintive wail.

Even the endless miles of white, the countless hours of wind in the face, had not grown boring or tiresome as Virginia rushed deeper into the Arctic, propelled by the huskies' powerful legs and Nick's masterful, big square hands. She had watched the wilderness whoosh past, glinting violet and silver in the moonlight. With each mile, with each rasp and skid of blade and click of paw on the ice, she had felt herself in the grasp of some kind of internal giddiness. Her life, the entire world, seemed to be spinning out of control. She found herself wondering if she would ever again set foot on steaming concrete or cushiony grass.

When the five travelers stopped, conversation was light, as if the long hours of silence had numbed the need to converse, even as tiredness and cold had numbed muscle and flesh. They set up camp. She fed the huskies, snatching her hand back quickly to avoid their snapping teeth. She walked and stretched. She joined the men in their small, tight ring and ate.

Seal again.

"Mesquite grilled," she had said as she swallowed yet another bite that was unrelieved by seasoning or sauce. "That would help."

The Akuchti had stared at her blankly. Nick had grinned.

"If you're going to fantasize, you might as well wish for filet."

"Or salmon. Delicate salmon, flavored with lemon butter."

"Salmon we can get. This spring, after the—"

He stopped suddenly and clamped his mouth shut.

She swallowed hard. "After what?"

"The thaw."

By then they should be back in Colorado. But she didn't say it and neither did he. She tried not to think about what Nick had said the night before. That they were caught up in something, that they had been dragged into this by some force they didn't understand.

She'd tried also not to think of his kiss, a kiss as head-spinningly powerful as their first had been.

Trying not to think of the kiss had been as futile as trying to visualize a warm tropical breeze and the smell of coconut oil. What she wouldn't give right now to slip into a bikini, stretch out in a canvas beach chair and feel warm coconut oil being worked into her back by Nick's big, broad hands....

She had gone to bed then. Not with Nick, as she had grown accustomed to in the past few nights. Which was just as well, given her state of body. Nick stayed with the Akuchti, who spoke in deep, slow murmurs once Virginia—the outsider, the woman—left them alone.

Set apart in the small tent, Virginia contemplated her restless body and wondered if it were only her imagination that the wolf wailed closer to home once the fire and the conversation died out.

She wondered, too, if Nick would finally join her now that the others had grown quiet for the night. She hoped he wouldn't, for the sake of her quivering nerve endings. She prayed he would, for the same reason.

He didn't. Only the lone wolf seemed inclined to come closer.

"Shut up," she finally ordered the beast, only to elicit a menacing growl from one of the nearby dogs.

Finally, acknowledging that her eyes were wide and her heartbeat far from calm, she crawled out of the tent. Standing, she looked around. The men huddled with the sled dogs for warmth. The fire smoldered, little more than a dot of gradually graying ash on the ice.

Snugly zipped and laced, she walked toward the only discernible landmark, a ragged jut of ice that was the beginning of a small mountain range a few hundred feet from where they camped. The range extended for miles; she had already learned enough about the way this terrain skewed perspective that she wouldn't hazard a guess how far the cliffs of ice extended. But here, at its beginning, she could walk to it and look around it, to the other side.

More ice, she knew.

On the off chance that this was some magic door into spring, she walked toward it. It was better than lying on her back in the darkness, thinking. Feeling. Fantasizing.

She had almost reached the jutting ice when she heard the crunch of footsteps behind her. Heart leaping, she whirled.

Nick.

"Don't sneak up on me like that."

"Did you think I was a mugger?"

She tugged her arms against her chest to control the shivering her fright had triggered.

"You could've been Mr. Wolf, coming up for a closer serenade."

"You shouldn't be out here by yourself."

She turned away to hide her irritation and her pleasure at seeing him. "I'm a big girl."

She heard him chuckle and raised her chin; it added an extra inch, she had decided years ago.

"If you're going to wander around in the wild, you'd better learn to keep your eyes and your ears open. You should've heard me long before I got this close."

She looked around at him. He had taken three more steps in her direction and was even closer now. Close enough to touch. Close enough to look him in the eye and let this crazy need of hers show. She turned away.

"You're right." She began to walk.

He fell in step beside her. "Is it getting to you?"

"No." His boots sounded confident on the ice; she tried to match his stride, to take the tentative sound out of her step on the ice. "Why should it?"

"It usually does."

They rounded the sharp corner of the range. On the other side, another sea of ice mocked her. She sighed.

"I was hoping for a tree," she admitted. "Maybe a sidewalk café with little red-and-white-striped umbrellas to keep the sun out of our eyes."

She laughed but knew it was a forlorn sound. He put his arm around her shoulder. She couldn't help it. The nearness of his body comforted her even as it exhilarated her. She gave herself up to the sensations. She pressed closer.

"How can you stand to do this?"

"Visit the Arctic in the dead of winter? I can't say that I've made a steady habit of it."

"But you're always traipsing off to some out-of-reach place. How can you do it? Does it always feel this...lonely?"

"Sometimes."

"Then why?"

"You hired me. Somebody always hires me."

"But it isn't that."

He was silent. She wanted him talking. She liked the deep confidence of his voice. And talking was safer than silence, when her thoughts might turn to another kiss.

She blinked hard, swallowed hard. "People in Sugarplum Bluff say you have an agenda."

"An agenda?"

"You want to save the world. You won't be hired by just anyone. Not trappers or hunters. Only scientists and environmentalists."

"And ladies in distress."

"I am not a lady in distress." But the little-girl part of every woman, the part that always wanted to believe in fairy tales, fluttered happily. It allowed her to revel in his deep voice, his solid chest, his nearness.

"Oh?"

"No. I'm a person on a mission." Again silence. "And so are you, Nick Closthaler."

His answer was to move his face close to hers. His lips brushed her forehead; they were soft and warm.

"Tell me about your mission, Nick," she whispered softly, uncertain which she wanted more, the continued intimacy of hearing his thoughts or the promised intimacy in the touch of his lips.

"You've already told me. I want to save the world."

"Then tell me why."

He was brushing his lips across the tips of her eyelashes. One hand cradled her head, drawing it close to his chest and face. The other lay possessively around her waist, searching, fingers pressing through the thickness of down for the contours of her body. Virginia longed to be wearing a single layer of supple silk.

"It started with my father."

Virginia's reporter's instincts came alive. Time for silky kisses and heated touches later. Maybe.

"Tell me about him."

He grew very still. "He was a logger."

"Yes?"

"He owned a lot of trees in Oregon. So he did what any red-blooded American businessman was supposed to do in his day." She felt the tension grip his body; his fingers tightened around the fabric of her coat.

"He harvested them?"

"He butchered the whole bloody forest."

She heard in his voice a bitterness she would have bet went far deeper than the frustration of a son who disagreed with his father's business practices.

"Is it your job to atone for that?"

"Somebody has to."

She decided to let it ride, knowing he wouldn't volunteer more without prodding. At least she knew something now; she could see a spark of light in the darkness that was the mystery of Nick Closthaler.

"And Virginia Holley asks her nosy questions because...?"

The bitter bite had disappeared from his voice, so she smiled at his gentle dig. "It's my job to know the answers."

"Why that job? Are you crusading, too?"

"Because it lets me find out about people's lives and yet...I can still be objective."

"You mean distant."

She felt an instant of defensive discomfort at his insight; perhaps she had liked him better when he was the strong, silent type. "I have to be distant. It's not my job to get involved. Just to report on what I see."

"So you can experience life vicariously."

"I do not experience life vicariously."

"You don't?"

She snuggled her face into the soft down crevice where the sleeve of his jacket met the shoulder. She tried to imagine the arm and the shoulder beneath; she wondered if they would ever get closer than these endless layers of clothing allowed. "Does this look vicarious?"

Their thighs pressed tightly together; she felt his breath, heard its ragged sound. "Could be."

"You're crazy." She wondered if he was aroused and resented being forbidden any telltale signs.

"Then prove me wrong, Virginia."

She raised questioning eyes to his and saw the answer she sought. Rising on her toes, she pressed her lips to his. The stubble he had allowed to grow during their days on the tundra was a prickly softness against her cheek, her chin, the edges of her lips. The frigid air swirling around them seemed to disappear in the vortex of heat eddying through their bodies.

"I want you, Virginia Holley," he whispered against her lips.

She wanted to whisper the answering words, but they stuck in her throat. If she said them, if she admitted out loud that she wanted him, too, wouldn't that ensure exactly what she dreaded most? Hadn't everything—everyone—she had ever needed and wanted in her life been snatched away?

The fear crept through her, cold and isolating, robbing her of the passion that had blazed so compellingly. She pulled away.

"We'd better go in."

She wouldn't look at him. She started walking back toward the tent, and eventually he followed. The wolf howled again, so close she almost missed Nick's gruff whisper.

"Running won't keep you from getting hurt, you know. Nothing can protect you from that."

VIRGINIA STORED her notes, clicked off her portable computer, snapped the screen into its closed position and stashed it in the orange vinyl bag atop the green vinyl bag that contained their supply of dried food.

The green bag, Nick had told her during their lunch break, contained enough food for five or six more days. It was December 17. If they didn't make it...

"Don't sweat it, Frosty," she whispered to the dark brown husky with the gray-ringed face who always held the spot closest to the sled. "If anybody can get us there, Nick can."

The animal turned baleful eyes on her. He had grown accustomed to her friendly tone and the nickname she had bestowed, a whimsy Virginia hadn't revealed to Nick or her stolid Akuchti guides.

"And if nobody can get us there?" she repeated in response to the dog's silent but expressive reaction. "Don't be ridiculous. Don't forget. This is Christmas. You always get your wish at Christmas."

After all there was no need to burden Frosty with her string of unfulfilled holidays past.

She glanced toward the group of men. Nick and the others were debating a change in course. The weather ahead looked ominous, Tom Elkhorn said with solemn authority. Virginia scanned the dark sky, where occasionally these days even the moon disappeared behind a bank of clouds, taking their only beacon with them.

"Even Mother Nature thinks this is a bad idea," Virginia had muttered the night before over yet another dinner of cold, hard salami and dried apricots.

Tom had looked alarmed. He had waved his left hand over his head and brought it to rest before closed eyes, an Akuchti symbol that was roughly the equivalent of a Catholic crossing herself in the face of danger.

"No," Tom had insisted. "Not discuss priestess of wilderness. She know."

All good reporters knew when to put a lid on it. Virginia made like a good reporter.

But when you looked into the brooding sky overhead, it was hard to believe Mother Nature—or the priestess of wilderness or auntie outdoors or whatever you wanted to call her—wasn't gearing up to rain a lot of grief down on their heads.

She walked toward the front of the sled Nick always guided, speaking softly to each of the wary dogs.

"Why, grandma," she crooned to the broadest of chest and longest of fang. "What big teeth you have."

The huskies seemed reluctant companions at first, but she was making headway. They no longer rumbled deep in their throats when she passed. Occasionally she felt certain their snouts tipped the air in a welcoming sniff.

"The better to munch me with?" she asked the next dog down the line.

When she reached the back of the sled, she looked at the stand where Nick would take his position within the quarter hour. She always envied him that moment of power, that moment of being in command, when he stood there and unleashed the strength of the dogs. The wind bit into his face bitterly, she knew, sometimes tearing his eyes despite his goggles and depositing frost on the springy curls peeking from the hood of his coat.

But how alive he must feel!

Glancing around the sled at the men deep in a pow-wow, Virginia put one hand gingerly on the hand rest. It felt solid. Emboldened, she put one foot into place, then another. She gripped the handholds, taking care not to disturb the reins resting there.

She looked out over the broad backs of the huskies and the shimmering expanse of ice and imagined herself in command of it. The excitement filled her lungs.

Being a reporter was exciting sometimes—when you weren't tracking down the next sewer-rate hike at city hall. But not this exciting. Not as exciting as it would be to fly through the air—feet firmly on the ground, of course—with hundreds of pounds of power beneath your fingertips.

A long, menacing howl startled her. She responded to the distant cry with a scrambling clutch of the handholds. Her fingers tangled in the reins, jerking them.

And the hundreds of pounds of power beneath her fingertips responded.

Virginia barely managed to hold on as the team of dogs, spooked at first by the howl of the wolf and next by Virginia's clumsy tugging on the reins, dashed across the ice. Firsthand Virginia felt the biting wind she had just been imagining. Except she had no goggles and could only clench her eyes tightly shut.

She refused to scream. Girls screamed. Flighty wisps of women screamed.

Virginia Holley, ace reporter, didn't scream.

At least, not out loud. But inside her head, she was howling just as loudly as the wolf who had caused this whole catastrophe.

With trembling fingers, she clutched the flying sled, barely able to hold on against the escalating speed, barely able to hold her position against the force of the wind at her face.

Even Nick couldn't do a darn thing for her now. The realization almost wrenched a frightened little squeak out of her, but she gulped it down.

Nick. What would Nick do in this spot?

Gain control. Show the huskies who was boss.

Right, Holley. And he'd do that with the extra sixty-five pounds of muscle at his disposal.

She slitted her eyes. A sheer peak of ice loomed on the horizon. She wondered if someone up front would have the presence of mind to detour.

Gain control. To gain control she would have to take a firm grip on the reins. To take a firm grip on the reins, she would have to release her death hold on the armrests.

She wondered how much damage would be done if she flew off the back of a sled going what felt to be at least seventy-miles per hour.

Taking another peek, she countered that concern with the thought of how much damage would be done if she flew straight into the side of the approaching cliff.

Still grasping the armrest with her right hand, she slowly, inch by inch, released her grip with her left hand. Then, in one swift dart, she raised her free hand and grabbed at the reins. Missed. Steadying herself, she grabbed again. Connected with leather. Wavering in her stance, she jerked on the left rein. The team responded with dizzying speed, jerking to the left and almost sending her flying off her precious perch. When she steadied herself again, she drew a long, deep breath and grabbed the right rein in her right fist.

The dogs felt the pull and straightened their course, which was at least several yards to the safe side of the sheer cliff. But they were still roaring along at a pace that threatened to buffet Virginia right off her feet.

Partial control. She felt it tingling in her fingertips. She felt it zipping from her mind to Frosty's. It gave her courage.

She whipped the reins around her wrists.

Good plan, she fretted. *Now, if you fall, you won't just hit the ice with a crash. You'll be dragged.*

Reins now held firmly, she pulled.

The spooked animals resisted her lightweight tug.

She had to get all her weight—such as it was—behind the reins. So she did the only thing she knew to do. She leaned back. Way back. Digging her feet in, her hands and wrists cut by the leather reins, she leaned far back from the sled.

And finally, when she had just decided she couldn't hold her position another forty-five seconds, the team began to slow.

She straightened, cutting the slack on the reins by whipping the leather around her wrists another couple of times. The three hundred pounds of power slowly bent to her will. She felt stronger with each decrease in speed.

They slowed. And finally stopped.

Knees trembling, Virginia gingerly unwrapped the reins and laid them gently in place. She stepped out of position, only vaguely aware of the nervous perspiration slicking her body beneath its layers of warm clothing, and staggered away from the sled. Her heart was racing out of control, and she felt certain she had left her stomach several miles back on the ice. She stumbled against the cliff of ice they had barely missed and sagged against it, eyes closed, heart dangerously in overdrive.

It was some moments before her breath stopped roaring in her ears, before she was aware of anything except her exhilaration and fright. Before she was aware of the scent of something unfamiliar—and wild—beside her.

She opened her eyes to discover a giant white wolf staring intently into her face.

Chapter Seven

To his team gave a whistle...

His eyes mesmerized her.

She couldn't move a muscle, and it was more than fear riveting her in its grip.

The white wolf's eyes were a gray so translucent they almost disappeared against the lush ruff of fur ringing his massive head. Those eyes didn't waver, and nothing wild surfaced in his steady gaze. Instead, his magnetic eyes looked deeply into her.

They held no menace.

Of course not, you twit, she told herself between painful breaths. *He's not afraid of you. You're about as threatening to him as a rabbit.*

To flee, she knew, would be folly. He would have her ankle in one swift snap of that long, elegant snout. She was facing down death with absolutely no gracious way out.

Ozzie will pay for this. An icicle-covered ghost will haunt him the rest of his life. And into the next one.

He was larger than her, easily more than one hundred pounds of muscle and lush white fur. He was beautiful in his power and in the majestic certainty with which he studied her face.

And strangely he didn't look inclined to gobble her up for lunch.

Delusions, she assured herself. *You're already having delusions.*

She had to try something. Maybe she could back away. Slowly. Quietly. He might not notice. He might not even be hungry.

Right. And there might be a Santa out there waiting for you to catch up with him, too.

Nevertheless, inaction was inexcusable.

She moved her left foot backward half a step, taking care to crunch on the ice as little as possible. The clunk of her boot sounded like the beginnings of an ice avalanche.

Mr. Wolf cocked his head to one side; his eyes grew curious.

She waited, and when he didn't seem instantly inclined to pounce, she moved the other foot.

Too bold. Mr. Wolf nosed forward. He snuffled at the front closure of her jacket. Virginia closed her eyes tightly.

Let it be fast. At least let it be fast.

The touch of his nose vanished. She peered out. He had backed away a step himself and was settling on his haunches to watch her.

"Oh!"

He acknowledged her sound with a mewling rumble in his chest that sounded almost friendly.

"Well," she whispered. "In that case, if it's all right with you..."

And she backed away. One step. Another. Eyes never leaving the wolf, she groped her way toward the sled and stepped into position. Mr. Wolf simply stared benevolently as she snapped the reins and set the team of huskies in motion.

NICK COULD BARELY KEEP his mouth shut as he watched Virginia guide the sled to a gentle halt beside the team he had been leading frantically to her rescue—with no idea how he was going to manage such a feat. He had seen plenty of Westerns, and he wasn't sure he could manage John Wayne's heroic jump onto the back of a runaway stagecoach team.

But he'd been willing to try. The thought of something happening to Virginia had been enough to wipe every rational thought right out of his head.

Just as he'd feared. She endangered them because he didn't show good judgment when she was around.

But she'd saved herself. At least he'd thought so until he watched, from almost a mile away, as she stumbled off the sled and into the path of the giant white wolf.

He had been ready to snap his team to top speed, even though he had no notion of being able to reach her in time. Then he saw that the wolf seemed mesmerized by Virginia, caught up in the trusting blue gaze that had certainly brought Nick to his knees.

When she walked away while the wolf watched with undisguised fascination, Nick knew with a certainty that Virginia Holley was indeed a force to be reckoned with. And he was in way over his head. Some things a man was absolutely powerless over.

She pulled her sled up alongside his.

"Where are you going?" she asked, her voice teasing despite the breathless edge he recognized from his own experiences in walking away from what had looked like the jaws of certain death. Something in her voice, her face, her stance, excited him.

"I thought I was going to have to play hero."

She turned that dimpled smile on him, and he was pleased with how tickled she was with herself. Damn, it was nice to be standing here, sharing the brightness of that smile.

"Guess I managed okay myself."

He saw the subtle squaring of shoulders.

"I guess you did." Then he remembered. She had been in danger, and the very thought of it aroused powerful emotions in him. "But I still ought to tie you to the sled for that little stunt."

Her dimples disappeared in the wake of the stubborn glint in her eyes. "Well, you can hardly think I did that on purpose."

"No. I think you did it out of carelessness."

"Is that so?"

"And there's no room for carelessness up here, Virginia." He wanted to take her in his arms and shake some sense into her.

"I am not a child, and there's no need for you to treat—"

"I'll treat you like one when you act like one."

Only he didn't feel like treating her like a child at all. He felt like reaching across the cold, arid air that separated them, grabbing her halo of silky blond hair with his gloved fist and pulling her to him. He wanted to crush those petulant lips with his, wanted to reassure himself with her warmth, wanted to feel the electric strength he knew was pulsing through her right now. He had experienced enough danger to remember the arousal that always followed.

Yes, the arousal always followed, even, it seemed, when you only experienced the danger secondhand.

"I want you." He surprised himself with the darkly growled words.

She was momentarily silent. He saw but couldn't hear the little shudder of breath she expelled. "Now?"

"Right now. Right here."

Her tongue peeked out to moisten her lips; her eyes were locked into his. "Oh."

The breathless little response intensified his fantasy, carrying his arousal to the next level. He could see her, on the ground.... "Legs around my waist..."

He didn't realize he had spoken aloud until he heard her gasp.

"And the moonlight on your breasts..."

"Oh. Well."

Her eyes grew fuzzy; so did her voice. She gulped. So did he. They were silent for a long time. He wondered if she were envisioning his words as vividly as he was.

"Nick, I...um..."

He watched as she moistened her windburned lips with the tip of her tongue. It was blush pink. His need was a painful ache, and it made him angry with himself. Angry with her. He twisted his face into a ferocious frown.

"But I can't afford to be careless, too," he snapped.

He was instantly sorry. He saw the blurry-eyed passion in her face shift to instant defensiveness. Her chin edged upward, her lower lip—that full lower lip that had been known to soften sweetly against his—jutted out stubbornly.

"It's your thinking that's getting careless, Closthaler. If you think I'm going to fall into your lap, I'm afraid you'll be waiting around *way* longer than the spring thaw. Now, if you'll excuse me, I have to get back to camp," she announced. "That is, if you think I can handle the team."

And she took off, a bit faster than she had approached him. Groaning against the uncomfortable strain at the front of his pants, and the damned foolishness he had just spoken, Nick followed, all the while calculating the time to the spring thaw.

TOM ELKHORN WATCHED the interplay between White Hunter Nick—a name he had never understood, since he had never seen the barrel-chested white man in possession of either a gun or the kind of knife that would be useful in tracking bear or caribou—and the Sun Woman Virginia Holley.

Ringing the evening fire, the two sat at opposite ends of the circle. They did not look at each other, yet their attention never strayed. Nick felt her presence, and she his. Elkhorn knew enough of man-woman games to understand that. Man-woman games, he could see, were much the same even in the white man's world.

Yet there were differences. They had not spoken when the journey continued, following the woman's rendezvous with the white wolf. Nick had manned his sled as usual, although his mouth was set more stubbornly, his expression easily read despite the beard he'd acquired after nearly a week in the wilderness. And, although she had previously ridden only with Nick, the woman had marched to Elkhorn's sled and requested transport in that determined way no Akuchti woman would dare assume. More like the way a polar bear claimed a freshet as his own after the thaw. More boldly than was seemly.

Elkhorn had debated his course of action. Should he wait for Nick's approval, the woman being his? Or should he simply nod in the way of the white people?

No matter. She had climbed atop his sled without waiting for approval. Elkhorn had looked at Nick with only the corner of his eye. And he had not been surprised when Nick came to debate the issue of her transport with the woman.

"You're overburdening Tom's sled," Nick had said with briskness. "Get back where you belong."

She had glanced then at Elkhorn. He gazed at the horizon, not seeing anything.

"I need a change of scenery."

"Welcome to the Arctic. You won't get much variety."

The sparring interested Elkhorn, although he did not let it show. He had not seen such between a man and his woman.

"I am not going to ride with you just to give you a better chance to think about my... legs. And other things."

Elkhorn pretended not to notice Nick's irritably embarrassed glance in his direction.

"I am not thinking about your... anything."

She harrumphed in a way that said she was not to be easily convinced of Nick's protestations. Wise woman. Elkhorn was not easily convinced, either.

"Besides," she said, "you haven't shown much consideration for what I just went through."

"You mean nearly losing our sled? You mean risking our best team? Excuse me, I forgot how traumatic it must have been."

"I could be dead. And I think you should do something about it."

"I offered to tie you to the sled."

She glared at him, but Elkhorn detected something less than genuine animosity in her eyes.

"Maybe you could make like the macho warrior. Kill the big bad wolf and . . ."

"No!"

Now all were surprised, including Tom Elkhorn. Certainly he had not intended to intrude. But when she spoke of the white wolf . . . All looked at him with questions in their eyes.

"You cannot kill white wolf."

He saw in her eyes she did not really want it so, anyway. Then Elkhorn understood this comment of hers was another part of the battle between man and woman, a part he did not understand.

Still, she spoke against his words. "It's dangerous. It could have killed the huskies and me."

Nick waited.

Elkhorn shook his head. "You cannot kill white wolf."

Nick then turned to glare at Virginia victoriously. "You see?"

"I see that you men are all alike. Stubborn and opinionated."

The man-woman argument ended when she gave in and stalked away to her usual post in Nick's sled. The journey continued.

When the day of travel came to its end and the woman went about her task of caring for the animals—a task Elkhorn had at first been reluctant to entrust to the pale-eyed woman with the hands and feet of a child—she edged close to him as he unloaded supplies for the night.

"Why not? Why shouldn't we kill the white wolf?"

Elkhorn looked into her eyes and only then did he decide to reveal what he knew.

"You have looked into white wolf's eyes."

She nodded.

"What did you see?"

She hesitated. "He was...curious."

"It is because he wonders why you have been granted safe passage."

"What?"

Elkhorn shrugged. "White wolf knows. He lives here for many Arctic winters. Hundreds of Arctic winters."

"Hundreds? But that's not possible."

Elkhorn merely nodded. "He follows us."

"Follows us?" A note of panic crept into her voice. "Stalks us?"

"Not stalk. Protect. Guard. White wolf is omen."

She opened her mouth to protest but did not. Elkhorn turned away, concerned that he had said too much to the woman, who should know only what was necessary anyway.

"How did you know we were coming, Tom?"

Elkhorn walked away without turning back. Yes, he had said too many things. The woman did not need to understand what he knew of the spirit world and the way the spirit world spoke to him.

What she needed to know about the spirit world, she would learn in her own time.

Chapter Eight

And mama in her kerchief . . .

Theodore dumped his mauve-and-gray tapestry luggage—filled to bursting with thermal long johns, insulated socks, fuzzy earmuffs and various other necessities for the North Pole–bound—onto the parqueted floor of the foyer.

Then he cooled his heels. Tapped his toes. Checked his watch.

Mother Nature, he had been warned, always kept her supplicants waiting.

Theodore didn't like the idea that he was being received as just another supplicant. Surely she remembered the time he had helped her with that avalanche in 1909 when that explorer Peary and his men were dangerously close to discovering the Toyland Compound. He had been of invaluable assistance. *She* owed *him,* and not vice versa.

Nevertheless, he supposed her slights would have to be endured until he moved up the hierarchy, into his rightful position atop the globe.

Mother Nature. M.N. to her intimates. He remembered vividly the only time he had actually seen her. At that intergalactic conference of myths and legends. And there, amid teeming crowds of leprechauns and genies and unicorns, M.N. had paled them all. The woman had presence.

That doesn't, Theodore fumed, *excuse tardiness.*

By the time the silk curtains parted and a curl of scented mist beckoned him to M.N.'s little hideaway here at the base of the Bermuda Triangle, Theodore was in one of his snits. He was going to have to do his best to hide it.

Her softly lit sanctuary looked like a sheikh's harem. Decadently plump pillows, all of a size for langorous reclining, were tossed hither and yon. Gauze draped the walls, and silk curtains fluttered around a stack of pillows piled higher than all the others. Her throne.

As his eyes rested once again on M.N., all Theodore's animosity vanished. She was even better than he remembered.

"Make yourself comfortable, Teddy."

Her voice was a breathy whisper. And she remembered his name, which thrilled him until he recalled that M.N. remembered everything. Unlike the old goat at the North Pole, she didn't even need a computer to keep track of it all, either.

Theodore sat cross-legged on one of the champagne-colored cushions at her knee. M.N. lay back on her satin pillows, her breasts billowing provocatively above the loosely laced bodice of her gown. Her hips and belly were lush in that delicious way real women once were. Her hair was a nimbus of platinum waves. Her eyes were heavy lidded, her mouth full and red.

"What brings you all the way to Mom's Place today, Teddy?"

"I need your help, Mother Nature, in an endeavor that I'm sure is close to both our hearts."

She studied her toenails, wriggling them so candlelight glinted off the red enamel. Theodore waited for her response until it became obvious she was waiting for him to continue. "I'm sure you've heard Kris Kringle's plans."

She nodded so slightly he almost missed it.

"He's bringing in two—" he mustered the necessary effort to keep from sneering the word "—humans to fill his role."

He hoped for some reaction. She merely raised one of her perfectly arched eyebrows. He wondered how she achieved that look.

"This can't be allowed to happen," he asserted.

"Oh?"

"They're humans!" Despite his resolve, Theodore's illusion of dispassionate objectivity slipped. He leapt to his feet and paced. "You know what a mess humans make of things! Look at the rain forest! Look at the ozone layer! Look at the homeless and the chemical warfare and the humpback whale!"

"You realize, Theodore, that they won't be humans for long. As soon as they reach the pole, they'll be given the power."

Theodore felt the vermilion creeping up his face and ears and was powerless to stop it, Elfin Elixir or no.

"Mother Nature, this isn't right. I was groomed. I was the chosen one. The old man has lost it. Completely. He's picked some woodchopper's son instead of me."

"Exile has not improved your temperament, Teddy."

Completely frustrated, Theodore flopped once again on the cushion at her knee.

"This defies every rule you stand for, Mother Nature. Taking a human and..."

She raised a hand, all hint of seduction now gone from her eyes.

"Just tell me what you want, Theodore. I don't need your campaign slogans to make up my own mind."

"You can stop them, Mother Nature. They're under some protective shield, or they never would have made it as far as they have in the Arctic. But such protection is powerless, if Mother Nature decides to intervene. You can stop them. You can end this travesty."

He held his breath, expecting her to ponder, to give due consideration. But she spoke quickly, even brusquely.

"Thank you, Theodore. Have a nice journey."

He was dismissed. And not even as nicely as Kris had dismissed him after that bungled coup attempt a few years ago. He stood, stung.

"But will you? Will you help?" He told himself there was no need for panic.

"You will know when it's time for you to know."

"With me in charge, we could make Christmas over, Mother Nature. We could put an end to all this Yule foolishness. Get rid of this magical, sentimental claptrap. Your law should prevail!"

She smiled. "It will, Theodore."

Despite her tone, her last words were reassuring. He left quietly and, as he boarded the private plane he had chartered, Theodore felt his confidence return. She had said what he needed to hear. Mother Nature's laws would indeed prevail.

Theodore knew Mother Nature's promise could mean only one thing: Kris Kringle's sappy, magical way of doing business was on its way out. History. Kaput.

NICK SPOTTED the white wolf before anyone else. He thought at first he should raise the alarm, it was trailing them so closely. But something kept him from speaking. He merely watched.

No matter how fast or how slow they traveled on this day—he checked his watch to discover it was already the nineteenth of December—the wolf kept them in his sights. When they slowed, he slowed. When Nick stepped up the pace, the white wolf did the same. When they stopped for lunch, he sat on his haunches a few hundred yards away, watching.

Nick was surprised when the next person to notice the animal's presence wasn't one of the Akuchti, but Virginia.

"That's him," she said as they packed away the few supplies they had pulled out for the brief lunch break.

He didn't have to ask who. He knew she meant this was the same wolf she had met days before. He also knew she was right, but he wasn't sure he wanted to alarm her with that admission yet. "How do you know?"

He looked down when she didn't answer. Her round face showed perplexity but not distress at the wolf's nearness.

"His eyes. They're silver, you know. Like ice in the moonlight."

"Wolves are brown eyed." Again, he knew she was right.

"Not this one." She spoke with calm certainty. "And the way he looks at us. As if...I almost felt like he knew who I was, why I'm here."

"That's not very likely."

She nodded. "I know."

Then he capitulated. Their game of pretense that all was normal here was pointless. "How do you suppose he knows?"

"The same way the Akuchti knew."

Anxiety prickled at Nick's consciousness. Virginia now suspected some sort of hocus-pocus was going on, too. Both of them were straitjacket candidates.

Before their caravan could be readied to continue, Tom Elkhorn came to them, his face more solemn than usual. "Akuchti turn back now."

"Turn back?" The anxiety in Virginia's voice echoed the sudden escalation of apprehension in Nick's gut. "You can't turn back. Nick, tell him we still have miles to go. They can't turn back now."

"Why, Tom?"

"You will arrive safely. Our guidance no longer needed." The Akuchti leader's eyes turned toward the white wolf. "You have protect."

"The wolf?"

Nick put his hand on Virginia's arm to quiet her incredulous protest. For once she responded as he had hoped, with silence.

"You can't come with us, too?"

"Not needed. In one day's time, you will reach the territory. We cannot cross into territory."

"Territory? Nick, what is he talking about? What territory?"

"Akuchti no can cross boundary into North Pole."

Nick froze, and he felt Virginia do the same at his side. "We're almost there?"

Tom nodded. "Tomorrow."

Virginia put her hand on Tom's sleeve. "What do you mean, you can't cross over into the North Pole?"

"Boundary not for all to cross."

"But we have to cross. Nick, we've come all this way. We have to cross over."

"You cross," Elkhorn assured her. "But Akuchti must turn back."

Nick nodded at the Native American guide who had been at his side through more than one safely completed expedition, then tipped his head in the direction of the wolf. "You say he's been sent to us?"

Tom Elkhorn nodded. "He is great white wolf. Overlord of Arctic for more than one century. If he guides you, nothing will harm."

Virginia threw up her hands and stalked off. "Overlord? Here to protect us? I'm sure Mother Nature would be pleased as punch to hear that little bit of lore."

THEY TRAVELED in the light of the waning moon, four dogs, one wild animal and each other for companionship.

"Funny," Virginia said to Nick. "I'm not afraid anymore."

You should be. Afraid to be alone with him again. Afraid of his pushing his way into her tent once again. Afraid of the way he couldn't keep his mind off her soft mouth and her soft body, and the way his body answered with uncontrollable hardness.

"It's the wolf," Nick said, but he didn't grin and neither did she. He hadn't expected her to.

"Are you afraid?"

Afraid to touch you. Afraid to answer the invitation I've seen in your eyes more than once the past few days. His thoughts spoke volumes, but he remained silent.

He looked up at the sky. Every twenty-four hours that passed shaved away another sliver of the full moon. And the sky brooded overhead. Even in the darkness, Nick could tell that the clouds billowing overhead were heavy with storm. He prayed it would hold off or blow over. Even the Akuchti's legendary white wolf was no match for a winter storm in the Arctic Circle.

But he wasn't about to share that bit of intelligence with Virginia. So he told her the dogs needed a rest. They could walk. Traveling slowly, he could keep his eyes open for some kind of shelter, in case the storm arrived.

"Tell me more about when you were little," she blurted out when they had settled into a comfortable walking pace.

He gave the barest of grins. "You're at it again."

"At what?"

"Grilling me. Playing reporter."

She wrinkled her nose in response. "I'm not *playing* reporter. I *am* one. So, tell me your life story and get it over with."

"Why do you want to know?"

"It's my job."

He looked down at her; her face wilted into sheepishness.

"Okay. That's not it. I ... I want to know ... I like to know what it was like ... for normal kids."

Her words, like everything about her, twisted at his gut, drawing out emotions he didn't want to deal with. And her face was so wistful, so vulnerable, he could make only two responses. He could cry. Or he could kiss her.

He wasn't about to cry.

"Virginia." He breathed her name as he brushed the side of her face with his damnably gloved hand. He leaned to her, bringing his lips to one wounded-looking eye, then the other. He intended to stop with that, but she breathed a sigh that he knew well enough meant desire.

So he put his hand to the back of her head and pulled her face up to his, covering her lips with his. He kept the kiss soft, gentle. If only he could make love with her now, he would be tender. He would wipe the wistfulness off her face.

The sigh that had escaped her lips, tempting him to a kiss, was now a moan in her throat. He felt the responding growl growing deep in his chest.

But when he heard the growl, it wasn't his. It belonged to one of the sled dogs.

Back to reality. Nick remembered the weather. He pulled slowly away. The regret in her eyes matched the protest trampling through his body.

"Um ... normal kid. Right. I'm ... uh ... not sure I was a normal kid."

"None of this is normal," she complained.

He stared into the endless, unchanging distance, registering the almost indiscernible escalation of the wind. "I know."

"But at least you had parents."

He glanced at her again, but her head was down. He couldn't see her eyes. All he knew of her mood was what he read into her lowered head, her drooping shoulders.

"Who took care of you?" he asked softly.

"Foster parents."

"Didn't you like them?"

"Which ones?" She looked up fleetingly to flash him a wry smile that he suspected was tougher than she felt.

"You had more than one?"

"Dozens."

He was engulfed by an aching need to make the hurt go away for a little Virginia Holley who had never really been part of a family. "What was that like?"

She grimaced. "Like being on the outside looking in. Say, you've done it again. I'm supposed to be the one asking questions here, not you. I want to know about your real live family with regulation parents and brothers and sisters."

"No brothers. No sisters."

She sighed. "Ah. Too bad. I always wanted a big family. Really big. One day—" She stopped abruptly.

"Me, too. One day."

"And your mother was...?"

"Overprotective." He could smell the storm now, could see the clouds roiling overhead. They would have to do something soon. But what?

"That explains your urge to run around the world putting yourself in danger. And your father?"

He shrugged. He tried to keep his mind on the ruthless terrain, to focus on some solution to the problem of the impending storm. But her talk of parents and childhood made it difficult for him to keep his mind on the business at hand. He remembered more than he wanted to; if not for his father, he wouldn't be here right now, trudging through a barren, frozen wasteland, responsible for the safety of a fragile, stubborn female, his only ally an untamed animal everyone insisted was a legend. If not for his father, might he be a satisfied accountant somewhere in middle America, with a wife and a station wagon and two point three kids?

But there was his father, and all his father had meant.

"The first time I saw a giant sequoia felled, I ran away from home," he said softly. "For two days, I lived in the woods."

"Why?"

"I couldn't...comprehend it. The tree was...it seemed sacred. Had been standing in that forest long before I was born. Long before my dad was born. It shouldn't have ended up shoved through a saw. It didn't belong in somebody's civilized, polished dining room."

Virginia put a hand on his arm. He looked down, first at the point where her hand brought fire to his flesh—even through all the layers of clothing—then up, to her eyes. He saw the fire reflected there, too. Their steps slowed. In a moment, he would have pulled her to him again, and Lord help them if a storm broke within the next few minutes.

As if she saw the danger in his eyes, she dropped her hand and spoke softly. "We didn't understand the things we understand now, Nick. Not in your father's day."

He nodded. "I know. I've told myself that. But we knew about treating human beings fairly. Even then we knew about that."

"What do you mean?"

"He kept his workers in poverty. And he endangered them every day. I..."

She prodded him when he hesitated. "What?"

"Nothing. He made me go to school with his workers' kids. Just to prove he didn't think we were better than them. But they all hated me. I wasn't ragged. Or hungry. My father hadn't lost a hand or died an early death because their father cared more about profit margin than safety. They hated me. And I hated him for it."

He felt her hand slip into his, then squeeze. As small as the gesture was, it helped. It eased the knots in his stomach that thinking about his father always brought.

"You're still trying to make it up to those kids, aren't you?"

"I suppose. I never really thought of it that way."

She nodded. "Trust me. Figuring out people is my job."

He grinned down at her. "I thought bullying them into answering your nosy questions was your job."

She grinned back. "Step one in the process."

Nick spotted the cloud sprinkling out its first flakes of icy snow at the same time he spotted an opening in the side of the ice cliff they walked beside. Up ahead the opening might reveal a cave large enough to protect them from the nasty storm that was brewing.

"Step it up," he said. "We need to hurry."

"Oh, look!" Delight filled her voice. "Snow! It's snowing! How wonderful! Can we—"

"We have to take cover."

He took her by the arm and started scurrying toward the opening. By the time they reached it, the snow had picked up. It was driving now, beginning to obscure their vision, already growing deadly. When Nick stuck his head in the opening to discover a deep cave, he heaved a relieved sigh.

"You stay in here."

"No. I'm going with you."

"I'm going to tie down the sled and—"

"I can help."

"You can help by staying out of this storm. It's deadly."

"Well, I'm not going to freeze to death in five minutes."

He heard the stubborn determination in her voice and groaned. "Maybe not. But you could lose your way. You don't know what it's like, how fast it can escalate. Now, stay put. You hired me to guide you, so do what I tell you."

"The deal didn't say anything about you getting to boss me around."

"You didn't read the fine print."

FOR TEN MINUTES, she sat on the floor of the cave, listening to the wind, watching the fire she'd built begin to flicker and glow, waiting for Nick to walk back through the narrow slit so she could fume at him some more about treating her like a child.

And after she had finished fuming at him, she would make sure they finished what they had left unfinished too many times before.

She planned to run her fingers through those springy curls that peeked out from beneath his stocking cap. She planned to find out just how abrasive those whiskers were against sensitive skin. Just how his chest was molded beneath all those blasted clothes. Whether he was noisy and joyful in his passion, or quietly intense.

As soon as he came in, she intended for the waiting and wondering to be over.

But he didn't come in.

After twenty minutes, she could take it no longer. She crept to the edge of the cave and peered out. What she saw drew a startled gasp.

What she saw was an impenetrable sheet of driving snow and ice. Mother Nature wreaking havoc. She couldn't see the sled or the team. She couldn't see the white wolf who had been their talisman of security for the past day.

And she couldn't see Nick.

Chapter Nine

A long winter's nap...

When Nick appeared at the narrow opening in the ice, Virginia was so glad to see him she flung her arms around his neck and hung on.

"Oh, Nick, I thought you were dead." She pressed a kiss to his cheek. Another to his forehead. He was safe! Nothing bad had happened to him. He was here, with her. Where he belonged. "I thought you'd finally gotten fed up with me and abandoned me to be eaten by great white wolves." She covered his cold neck with warm kisses. She might never stop kissing him. Never. "I thought— Good grief, you're frozen."

She stepped back. Icicles hung off his jacket, his gloves, his hat. Even the week's growth of beard was a matt of silver frost.

"You have to get out of those clothes," she said briskly, forcing herself to ignore the way her body was beginning to ache for his closeness. She reached for his hand and led him to the now-roaring fire.

"Can't."

"Sorry, Closthaler." She pulled his ice-encrusted cap off his head. She wanted to stop long enough to pull his dear, silvering curls tightly against her chest. Wanted, at last, to feel them beneath her fingers. Wanted to feel his cheek pillowed against her breast. But now was not the time for giving in to such weakness. "You may be Mr. Macho Expedition Guide when it comes to following the compass and securing the camp for the night, but when it comes to homey things like keeping warm and fighting off colds... Well, I may not have seen much mothering firsthand, but beneath this hard-bitten reporter's exterior lurks a world-class nurturer."

Even as she said it, she wondered if it were true. Right now, with this strong bear of a man, it certainly felt true.

"My change of clothes is on the sled," he protested, even as she was tugging off his gloves. "And if you think I'm going out there again, you're..."

"No, you most certainly are not going out there again." She rubbed his cold, stiff fingers between her palms. She wanted to touch her lips to every single fingertip. She paused for a moment, considering it, but she wasn't quite that brave. "Because I'm not letting you out of my sight again."

"You were worried about me?"

He made an effort to catch her eye, but she studiously avoided it. Couldn't afford to give away too much. Unless she already had. She bit her lower lip, silently cursing her impulsiveness. Just as she finished massaging his tenth finger, his hand broke free. He raised his thumb to the lip she had just caught between her teeth.

Yes, she had already given away too much.

Drawing a deep breath, she gave his thumb a playful bite. A low rumble sounded in his chest, which stirred an answering throb low in her belly. She cursed herself again. Another tactical error, that little bite. How she longed to grab him around the neck and kiss him soundly.

Instead, she pushed him to the ground and started unlacing his boots. "I have warm blankets right here, and we are going to hang these clothes to dry while you bundle up."

"But—"

"No arguing. A frostbitten guide is no use to me whatsoever."

"And to what good use are you going to put a warm guide?"

The low suggestiveness of his voice demanded that she look him in the eye. Never one to back down from a challenge, she met his eyes. And was instantly sorry.

Nick was aroused. As aroused as she. He smiled.

"Behave yourself, Closthaler," she murmured.

His first layer of clothes was already thawing out in puddles and dribbles by the time her shaky hands got them off and hung them near the fire to dry. Her heart was pounding, but she tried to concentrate on what she was doing.

And what, exactly, is it you're doing?

Unfortunately the driving ice had been too good a match even for his insulated outer layer—the pants and sweater he wore beneath were wet around the edges, as well. Mustering her courage, she started pulling his sweater up.

"Now, look, Virginia—"

She stared him straight in the eye and refused to back down. "Either you peel, or I'll do it for you."

She thought at first he planned to protest again. But as she watched, the humor in his eyes turned to surprise, then to anticipation. She tried to keep a straight face, amazed as her own anxiety melted into the same kind of anticipation she saw in his eyes. He leaned back against the wall of the cave and opened his arms wide. That first glint of good humor was heavy now with something else. Something that said he was willing to be seduced, if she were brave enough to play the seductress.

"I'm all yours."

He hadn't made the decision she had expected when she issued her ultimatum. Now, she knew, she would be forced to live up to her big talk. She relished the idea. Relished the thought of the game to be played.

Now he was grinning outright. He obviously didn't expect her to live up to her threat. And that was all the prodding she needed.

She finished pulling his sweater over his head, letting her palms linger over the swell of his chest. He was broad and hard beneath her hands. The longing in her deepened; the throbbing quickened. She started in on his shirt buttons. Briskly at first. After all, two layers of very serviceable cotton thermalwear lay beneath the thick red flannel. No big deal.

But her knuckles brushed his chest as she went along, grazed the hollow at the base of his throat. She felt the thump of his pulse, as rapid as her own, and the glow of his gradually rising body heat.

Then she hit his belt buckle.

Two choices. A delay tactic—tugging out his shirttail first—or right down to business—unbuckling for greater access. To the shirttail, that is.

Ozzie always told her a news story should get right to the point. "People aren't going to wait around to find out what you've got to offer 'em, Holley," Ozzie always growled as she changed her leads.

This was all Ozzie's fault to start with.

She went for the buckle.

Nick sucked his breath in, pulling his belly as far away from her touch as possible. She drew courage from the small sign of retreat and looked up at him through lowered lashes.

"Don't get squeamish now," she whispered. "It's going to get a lot worse before it gets better."

He didn't answer. He didn't let his breath out, either, until she let go of the buckle and finished with the snap at his waistband.

Courage, Holley.

She yanked on his zipper.

"Virginia—"

She reached up and covered his lips with one fingertip. "Hush. It's nothing personal, Closthaler. Strictly my angel-of-mercy routine."

But she tried to make sure he knew from the look in her eyes and the way her hands lingered oh, so lightly over separating his fly that she was thoroughly enjoying the game. From the way he swallowed hard and closed his eyes, she decided her message had gotten through.

She finished the buttons on his cuffs. Then she pushed his shirt off his shoulders, which were solid with muscle and gave off an alluring scent of man that momentarily dizzied her. She froze, poised over him, long enough to regain her equilibrium. This was nuts. What was she thinking, getting herself involved with this man who thought the only way to live was on the brink of danger. What was she thinking?

Don't think, she told herself. *Just feel. Just let yourself live. Just for this moment, just live.*

Her eyes were on a level with his lips. She remembered the feel of those lips, warm and soft even in the brittle Arctic. The dizziness spiraled through her, again. She laid the shirt carefully aside.

His pants came next. If he hadn't looked so confident that she'd never have the nerve to continue, she might have given up the whole game. But he did, so she didn't. Off came the pants.

She had no idea a man could look so virile in thermal long johns.

It might've had something to do with the way the stretch cotton molded itself to well-formed arm, chest and thigh muscles.

It might've had something to do with the way the fly of those long johns leapt and swelled in her direction.

"I think the underwear is wet, too," he said.

She'd never heard such a low, throaty laugh come from her lips in her entire life. "I don't think so."

He captured her arm with his hand before she realized what had happened. "And your clothes. Damp. Definitely damp."

"You're wrong, Closthaler." But she had no intention of protesting with any real vehemence.

"Who's the Arctic expert here, Holley?"

"You are, Closthaler."

"Then get out of those wet clothes. Now."

She did. Down to her long johns. He groaned as he watched and her fantasy dressed her in a satin push-up number and matching thong bikini.

Nick threw off his shirt. His chest glowed golden in the firelight, thick with light curls and powerful with muscle. She reached one finger across the darkness and scraped a nail gently across the pucker of one dark nipple.

He drew in a sharp breath. The sound squeezed her sharply in her lower belly.

She lowered her hand to his waistband, but he stopped her.

"Now you."

Thermal cotton disappeared as slowly and provocatively as if it were satin. Her flesh sprang to life, sensation rippling over her, as she felt herself touched so far only by his gaze. She was no longer afraid of what was happening.

He leaned over and traced the same line along her flesh that she had traced along his—except he did the job with the damp flicker of his tongue.

They cast off the rest of their clothing at the same time. His eyes never left her; hers never left him. Outlined in firelight against the stark white of the ice cave, he was quintessential, primitive male. Strong, forceful, undeniable.

In his presence, she felt herself the primordial female. Fertile, alluring, giving.

"This is how it should be," he said softly, making no move to touch her except for the way his eyes devoured every inch of her, over and over again.

She didn't have to ask what he meant. She knew. She felt it, too. "No games. No pretense. No false modesty."

"Just honest hunger."

Oh, yes, hunger. Her throat felt raspy. "Emotion."

"Love." Her instant of alarm must have registered in her eyes, because he shook his head in protest. "No games, remember? If it's love, that's what we call it."

Her mouth was dry now, too. But the openness in his face wouldn't be denied. She nodded. "Okay. Love."

He took the two steps necessary to bring their bodies together. His maleness grazed her belly, hot and hard. She wanted him to crush her to him, to satisfy the hunger raging in her with movements rough and rushed. But his touch, when he covered her breasts with the barest brush of his palms, was gentle. So gentle she cried out softly with the force of its power.

The power of love.

The thought almost frightened her into stepping back, into backing away from this moment. But she couldn't move. The emotion in his touch was stronger than her fear. So she stayed while his hands began to roam her body, caressing her breasts until they swelled and ached, sliding along her belly, exploring the curves of her hips, making every inch of her his.

Her head spun. She reached out to steady herself, one hand on his arm, the other against his chest. His hard, bare chest. Her fingers tangled in the thick, tight curls, found the tiny bead that was one taut nipple. He moaned and moved against her. She gasped, arched involuntarily. And he lowered one of his hands to explore her more intimately, finding the damp heat between her thighs.

She cried out, her fingers clutching, nails digging. The roar of the storm outside filled her body, raged within her.

"Now, Nick. I want you now."

With one hand, he lifted her face to his and looked into her eyes. "And I want you forever, Virginia."

He waited, all stillness. She saw in his eyes what he wanted. He wanted forever from her. But she wasn't that brave yet, and she wasn't willing to make even a silent promise without being sure she would keep it.

"What can you promise?" he asked.

The fear flickered again for a moment. His eyes stripped her too effectively; his touch drew all her emotions to the surface. Whatever she said would be naked truth.

"That I'll believe. In us. Wherever that takes us."

She saw in his eyes that it wasn't all he wanted. But he accepted it.

And with one swift, sure movement, he lifted her and brought her to him. Her legs encircled his waist. He lowered her. And they were one.

He held her there, breast against chest, bodies locked, without moving, holding her securely in his gentle grasp. Their eyes locked, caressed, spoke. Their bodies moved together, answering one another with a tender stroke, a trembling clinging. The fury of the storm within her had abated, had become a gentle rush of emotion and sensation.

Her lips grazing his, she whispered, "This is our..."

He sought her more deeply, cutting off her words, ending her thought with a gasp.

He finished the thought for her. "... our destiny."

No thrusting was necessary; her body coaxed his, his prodded hers. Their eyes kindled emotion to the point of smoldering combustion.

Then the flames licked to life. She exploded around him as he exploded deep within her.

When their trembling had stopped, he lowered her gently to the ground. She wrapped them in two thick, soft blankets. They lay cradled together, watching the fire, feeling the heat.

ELSA WAS EXPERIMENTING with the use of prune puree as a butter substitute to lower the fat content of her famous sugar cookies when Kris burst into the kitchen.

"Come with me, my dear," he said, taking the wire whip out of her hand and dropping it into the bowl of unattractive puree. "I have something I want you to see."

"Can it wait, Kris? I have this batter and—"

"Can't wait. Can't wait."

Grabbing a kitchen towel to wipe her hands as she whisked past a table, Elsa didn't bother to protest. When Kris got that twinkle in his eyes, there was little point in arguing with him. Sometimes he was as much a little boy as all the ones on his list.

"Whatever is it?" she asked as he led her into his office.

"You'll see. You'll see."

Then he pushed her in front of the Vista Master. Pulling her bifocals from her apron pocket, she plunked them on the end of her nose and peered into the screen.

She immediately turned red and snatched off her bifocals.

"Gracious' sakes, Kris! That looks like a man and a woman all wrapped up in a blanket together. What on earth do you mean, having me come in here for this!"

"Not just a man and woman, Elsa. Nick and Virginia."

Her mouth dropping open, Elsa held up her glasses and peered at the screen again. Sure enough, it was that nice-looking young man—he did look so much better now that his beard had filled out; when it silvered a bit more, in years to come, he would look even more dashing—and that darling little woman with the big blue eyes. Not that she could see the dear girl's eyes right now. They were closed. Her head was on his shoulder—which was quite well developed, Elsa noted in spite of herself—and they were sleeping like babes.

Well, not quite like babes. Truth be told, from the look of their bare shoulders over the blanket, they appeared to be quite entirely unclothed.

She blushed again, quite furiously, she was certain.

"Isn't that sweet?" Kris asked.

She turned to look at him. He was beaming at the screen, fairly popping his suspenders, he was so puffed up.

"Sweet? Gracious' sakes, Kris, they aren't even married."

He gave her a disparaging look. "A technicality, my dear. In spirit, they are married. And you know that matters much more."

"Well, I'm not so certain, Kris..."

"They're in love, woman. Where's your sense of romance?"

She looked back at the screen and had to admit there was something quite serene, almost spiritual, about the young couple lying there, protecting each other with their arms.

"Kris, you didn't spy on them—"

"Oh, mercy, no! They deserve a little privacy while they conduct their courtship, I should say. But I couldn't resist a little peek, and this is how I found them. Just wanted you to see. Wanted to set your mind at ease, Elsa, dear."

"I see."

And strangely the sight of them lying there did just that. Kris always had been a good judge of people. Well, except for that scoundrel Theodore. But that was ancient history.

She gave him a smacking kiss on one cherry red cheek. "Well, you were quite right, Kris. I'm sure everything is going to turn out just perfectly."

FROM HER ELEGANT LAIR at the base of the Bermuda Triangle, Mother Nature closed her eyes and concentrated on the Arctic Circle until her vision cleared.

Then she smiled.

Yes, the storm had done just what she had intended. The young couple lay snuggled together, talking and loving and discovering all the different ways their destinies were interwoven. She could see the healing of their lives' pain beginning, could feel hope blossoming in their souls.

And a few miles away, that silly twit Theodore sat stranded, using up even more of his precious supply of Elfin Elixir to survive one of those deliciously swirling, roaring, silvery storms Mother Nature did so love to send to her Arctic playground.

She smiled. All was well.

THE STORM RAGED for twenty-four hours.

"You'd think Mother Nature had some ulterior motive for locking us up here together," Virginia said, snuggling her cheek against Nick's chest and running one hand over the hard line of muscle from his back to his buttock.

"I'd say she's made a very wise move, then," Nick murmured, absorbing her touch, marveling at the power in something so gentle.

He knew they had only a few more days to reach their destination, but he was surprisingly unconcerned. They would make it. He knew that. Deep in his gut, where he usually made decisions when pitting himself against nature.

So he allowed himself to enjoy this interlude with Virginia. He allowed himself to wallow in the sheer pleasure of her soft, alabaster skin. He gave himself permission to run his fingers through the silkiness of her moonbeam blond hair, even as the moon lighting their way outside grew a bit dimmer with the passage of time. He buried himself inside her and felt her welcome him and knew this was exactly the way things were supposed to be.

"You could get pregnant," he said, remembering his responsibility even while basking in the afterglow.

"Don't. I don't want to think about tomorrow. About what could be."

"This whole trip is about tomorrow. All of our tomorrows." He wasn't sure how or why, but he knew he was right.

She shook her head. "Don't, Nick. Don't spoil it."

"Why does it spoil it, thinking about being together tomorrow and the next day and every other day after that?"

"Because...it's pushing your luck. To want it too much. To say it out loud."

And he remembered her life, a life in which every family she'd ever had had been temporary.

"I do want it too much," he said.

"Okay. But don't say it out loud." And she covered his lips with hers to assure he followed her orders.

As the storm entered its second twenty-four hours, the fury abated somewhat, and Virginia began preparations for leaving. Nick stood at the cave opening and looked out. The wind was less ferocious. The ice had ceased to pelt the ground, leaving only the soft drift of snow. And the moon had indeed grown alarmingly narrower in the dark sky. But the weather was still too dangerous to leave the safety of their cave.

"You needn't start packing up yet," he told her, turning back.

She faced him, her solid stance and set jaw telling him he was in for a battle.

"I have a story to finish. It's almost Christmas. And I've never missed a deadline. I don't intend to start now."

"This isn't about deadlines, Virginia."

He saw her hesitation.

"I still have a deadline, Nick. It's what I do. I have no choice."

"Yes, you do. No deadline is worth risking your neck."

She laughed. "If that were true, I wouldn't be here right now."

He felt himself growing angry as she grew more determined. "You'll wait till the storm is gone."

"I'll go right now. Alone, if I have to."

"Don't be a damned fool."

She turned then and, without saying a word, finished her preparations. When she was packed, she walked to the mouth of the cave.

"Come with me, Nick?"

He stood watching her, trying to convince himself there was no reason to be so afraid. She was fearless, he knew, but she wasn't insane. As soon as she got out into the final swirl of snow and wind, she would realize what she was attempting was impossible. She would come back.

She *would* come back. Of course she would.

When he didn't answer, she turned and stalked out of the cave. He waited. Forced himself not to follow her. She wouldn't get ten steps, he told himself, trying to squelch the panic welling up in his chest.

He wanted to stick his head out the door and scream after her. Just to see her.

She *would* come back. She *had* to come back.

He remembered the day they'd hit the tundra, the way she'd stalked off back into the woods. He'd found her leaning against a tree. Angry and wanting to be alone. He fixed that image firmly in his mind and reminded himself there was nothing to be afraid of.

He waited ten minutes. Then twenty. This was one stubborn woman he'd managed to get himself tied up with.

He walked to the opening and looked out once again on Mother Nature's fury.

No sign of Virginia. No sign of the white wolf.

He had never been so afraid of the Arctic as he was at that moment.

Chapter Ten

When they meet with an obstacle...

Stress always made Kris's feet hurt. And right now his big black boots felt a half size too small. Where were his bunion pads?

First and ever foremost, Elsa was fretting.

She had kept an anxious eye on Nick and Virginia and the howling storm that had slowed their progress the past two days. Always, of course, carefully tuning out when the young couple grew amorous. Then, just a few minutes ago, Elsa had zoomed in on the Vista Master just in time to see Virginia stalk out on Nick, although the raging storm had abated only marginally.

"Oh, dear," Elsa had murmured, her plump little hand fluttering near the pulse at the base of her throat. "Oh, gracious' sakes, Kris. This woman is going to get herself in grave danger, I fear."

Kris turned the contrast down on the screen, and the image of Virginia leaning into the frigid wind disappeared. "Now, Elsa. I've told you before, I've seen to all that. The white wolf is with her. And—"

"Can the white wolf protect her from her own stubbornness?" Nervously she pulled the doll production schedule out of her apron pocket and rolled it tightly in her fist. "Kris, you really should have consulted me before you made all these decisions. I do worry you've chosen a new Mrs. Claus who is a touch too independent. Had you spared a moment to consult with me, I could have told you—"

"Now, Elsa. Calm yourself." He put his arm around her shoulders, wincing as he hobbled beside her on aching feet toward the door. Better to get her away from the constant reminder that young Virginia Holley was indeed pushing the limits of what even Kris Kringle could protect her from. "It's a different world, Elsa. Women are more independent. It's the way of things. And you of all people know Toyland is no place for a wishy-washy woman."

She had been a little appeased when he finally ushered her out the door and on her way to the doll factory.

But peace and quiet to check the air currents for his route three days hence had not been forthcoming. Only moments after the door to his office closed behind Elsa, Noel had shoved his way into the room. His look was, if anything, more doleful than Elsa's had been.

"Kris, we have problems."

"Excellent. Excellent. Wouldn't want things to run too smoothly here less than a week before delivery," he grumbled. Yes, retirement could come none too soon for him.

In one nimble leap, Noel perched on the mantel and gazed down at Kris. "Testiness does not become you, Kris."

"Get to the point, Noel."

Noel folded his arms, uncurled his toes and studied the effect as they stretched out nine inches before him. Kris's opinion had always been that Noel was far too vain about the fact that he had the longest toes among all the Toyland elves. What he would do when the curl began to go limp—and the toes were always the first to go, it seemed—Kris didn't want to be around to witness.

The head elf finally looked up. "All the belts have snapped."

"What?" An urgent throb seized Kris's left big toe. "Which belt? Which assembly line is down?"

"All of them. Not one belt, Kris. All of them. Snapped." He snapped his fingers. "Like that."

"That can't be. Not all of them. The maintenance crew just checked all the assembly lines for parts that needed replacing last week. They could have missed one bad belt. But not all of them."

"I know, I know." Noel shook his head, a frown notching his tiny forehead. "But right before we finished the no-assembly-required line yesterday afternoon—with two hundred thousand leftover size-J wing nuts nobody could account for, by the way—the belt snapped. Then another one in doll-hair weaving. And another in teddy-bear buttons. Gezochstehagen started checking and discovered belts were snapping right and left. And the ones that hadn't snapped were ready to go."

Kris limped to his chair and flopped into the well-worn leather. "But that's impossible."

"Every single assembly line belt, dead, dead, dead."

Kris felt worse than uneasy; he felt close to giving in to panic. He looked up and saw the same feeling reflected in Noel's little amber eyes. "What do we do?"

"I called the moveable-parts crew in to help. We're replacing the belts as quickly as elfinly possible. With any luck and double shifts, we'll have everything moving again by midnight."

Kris nodded, propping a foot on his knee and massaging the dull ache spreading from big toe to fallen arch.

Noel spread his arms. "But if we don't know how this happened in the first place..."

"We'll do a quality-control check the first of the year. I'll put it on the calendar."

Noel gave a graceful hop and floated to the floor. Before his chief assistant started to the door, Kris said, "One more thing. What's the latest on Theodore?"

"Actually, Kris, we don't have much right now."

Now a twinge ricocheted through the middle toe on Kris's other foot. Kris knew he sounded querulous, but there was no help for it. "What in the name of wilted mistletoe does that mean?"

"It's the storm. Nobody can keep up with him in the storm. The Akuchti lost him. The radar might as well be operating through eggnog. He's ... vanished."

Kris eased his feet onto his padded footstool. "How can an elf whose favorite attire is sequins and rhinestones disappear? Without his Elfin Elixir, he's powerless. This isn't supposed to happen."

Noel's face crinkled up in a sheepish expression Kris found decidedly suspicious. "What is it, Noel?"

"Well, boss, about the Elfin Elixir..."

Without thinking, Kris bolted upright and slammed his momentarily forgotten feet to the floor. "You can't mean to tell me that little megalomaniac has gotten his hands on the elixir! Tell me that isn't what you're about to say, Noel!"

"We think it was Roxanne, boss."

"Roxanne?"

"She disappeared a few weeks ago. We thought she'd just headed off for another one of her trysts with that little troll she met last year. You know she's prone to do that. But she never came back. Then we noticed someone had been tampering with the elixir supply and...that's when we heard Teddy was on the move."

Kris groaned. Loud. Then louder. "So Theodore could be anywhere."

"He could be at Goose Bay, boss," Noel said, a note of hope in his squeaky voice. "You know, waiting for transportation."

Kris gave his assistant a baleful look.

"Or on the tundra," Noel continued. "Holed up somewhere, waiting for the blizzard to pass, like Nick and Virginia."

Kris slipped his feet into his loose, down-filled slippers. "Right. Or he could be right here in Toyland, plotting ways to sabotage batteries and moveable parts and accessories."

Noel turned an alarming shade of ocher.

"Get me a meeting, Noel. I want the best elves we have. The bravest. The most loyal. No more than ten, I think. We need to keep this quiet. But it's time to go on the offensive."

ONE OF VIRGINIA'S foster fathers had been fond of calling anyone who did something abysmally stupid a chowderhead.

Right now she could hear his voice echoing in her head. *Chowderhead.* It was dim, of course. As much as the storm had dissipated, it still raged on more ferociously than anything she had ever seen. *Chowderhead.*

And here she was, trudging through the ice and wind alone.

Well, almost alone.

There was the click-click-click of wolf paws on the ice behind her.

Unsure which direction they had been heading when the storm came on, Virginia had started off uncertainly after storming out of the cave. Only sheer, mule-headed pride had kept her from returning before she ventured twelve steps.

In the forty minutes since then, the only thing that had kept her from returning was the fact that she had no blooming idea which direction she had come from. Keeping her bearings in the blowing snow and wind was an utter impossibility. And, of course, she had been too angry when she left to think of mundane matters like compasses.

Actually, she had to admit, her motivation had probably been less anger than it had been fear. Fear that she was growing too dependent on him and the emotional high he produced in her. Even now, all she had to do was think of Nick and their lovemaking for the euphoria to strike. All the memories were too vivid: the thick, corded muscles along his arms and his back; the silky dampness of his tongue loving all the secret parts of her; the crisp hairs of his thighs against her thighs; the strangled cry he made each time his passion erupted.

It was all too scary. She was getting too close. And if she did indeed get too close, wouldn't Nick disappear? The way everyone else she had ever tried to label family in her life had disappeared?

Chowderhead.

No time for that. There was time only for keeping her feet, for heading straight ahead—as if she knew where straight ahead would lead.

The only reason she hadn't collapsed in a fit of screaming terror was the click-click-click on the ice behind her.

The white wolf had followed. She hadn't even realized that their wild companion had stayed nearby throughout the storm. And she hadn't seen him when she left the cave. But within a few minutes, she had sensed a presence. Expecting Nick, she had turned to see the white wolf over her shoulder. He followed, growing closer whenever the snow grew so heavy it threatened to obscure their vision of each other. His smoky eyes connected with hers whenever she glanced around.

Each time she did, Virginia felt her courage replenished. The wolf's eyes were the same dark color passion brought out in Nick's eyes.

She glanced back now for the reassurance and the memory. When she did, her right boot hit a chunk of ice. Thrown off balance, she hit the ground with a thud.

Her backside must not have been the only thing to hit the ice soundly. When she tried to stand, she felt slightly dizzy. Holding herself perfectly still for a moment, Virginia had to resist the urge to think how much more comforted she would be with Nick beside her right now. With Nick's arms around her. With Nick's chest solid and trustworthy beneath her cheek. With Nick's body ready to show her that even Virginia Holley could find love.

After all, Nick hadn't abandoned her. She had abandoned him.

Recovering her pack, she started out again. But before she had taken three steps, the white wolf stepped into her path. Not two feet from her, he faced her implacably, unmoving and immovable.

"Oh. Hi. Not to worry. I'm fine. Just a little spill."

Despite herself, she was nervous. After all, the only reason she had to trust this beast not to gobble her up for lunch was the Akuchti fairy tale that he was somehow the protector of all that was good and noble here in the Arctic Circle.

Tell that to Red Riding Hood.

She took another step. The wolf moved more determinedly than before into her path. When she tried to sidestep him, he moved to block her way.

"Now, listen, pal," she said, beginning to wonder if the wolf had indeed decided she wasn't going to get any plumper and juicier out here on the tundra. Was lunchtime at hand?

But when she looked into his silver eyes, nothing could persuade her that the white wolf meant her harm.

Nevertheless, he wouldn't let her pass. He kept moving to block her progress, and she kept moving to get around him, until she was pointed a hundred and ninety degrees in the opposite direction.

Then, and only then, did the white wolf step back and let her continue.

Mouth open, Virginia stared at him. "Is that it, pal? I was turned around? Going the wrong way?"

The wolf stared at her patiently, waiting for her to proceed, keeping his motives to himself.

With a shiver that started deep inside and had nothing to do with the cold, Virginia started walking. Now the wolf didn't retreat to walk a comfortable distance behind her. He matched her step by step, loping along at her side like a friendly bowser out for a walk in the park.

"What's this all about, pal?"

The answer filled her head. It was about the fact that she was needed, required in some way, at the North Pole. She had a role to play this Christmas. That much was clear.

"If I believe that, it makes me a candidate for a nut farm. Right, pal?"

The white wolf was a beast of few words.

They walked along, Virginia regaling the wolf with some of her best scoops during her reporting career. When she was in the middle of the episode with the sleazeball who bilked little old ladies of their life savings in return for worthless nursing-home insurance, the wolf suddenly nudged her gloved hand with his nose.

Startled, Virginia flinched away. The wolf nudged again, more insistently this time.

"What is it, pal?"

He flung his powerful head in the direction they had just come. Worry threaded its way into Virginia's consciousness. "Nick?"

The white wolf turned back, his eyes reproachful. The urge to protect grew strong in Virginia as she thought of Nick and wondered if he were in trouble. What if he were hurt? What if her foolhardy stubbornness meant she would never again have the chance to feel the rise and fall of his chest when they slept? Never again feel his kisses change from tender intimacy to fierce demand. She needed those things. Now. And forever.

"He's alone, right? He needs us."

The wolf retraced their tracks in the snow, then returned and stood by Virginia again.

"And we need him, too."

Acknowledging the truth of it, Virginia turned back in the direction the wolf urged.

In a matter of moments, a bulky figure appeared ahead of her through the blanket of falling snow.

Without doubting what she was throwing herself into, Virginia ran toward the shadowy figure and flung herself into its arms.

The arms settled around her familiarly, protectively.

"You're a crazy woman, you know that?" Nick whispered softly. "It isn't safe to be too fearless, Virginia."

When she looked up into his face, she saw the respect in his eyes despite the chiding in his voice.

When their lips met in a long, slow kiss, the storm stopped as instantly and completely as if someone somewhere had suddenly shut off the faucet.

THE ABANDONED FIRE in the cave was still smoldering when Theodore and Roxanne arrived. Livid, he kicked at the coals.

"Gone! Too late again!"

"Maybe we should forget them, Teddy. Get on to the compound and work this thing from inside."

"You are not the brains in this operation, Roxanne. Just remember that."

Miffed, Roxanne snarled at him. "*Is* there a brains in this operation? I hadn't noticed."

"Shut up. I have to think."

And he paced. He could smell the humans who had been here so recently. The very idea of coaxing humans up to Toyland merely proved how very senile the old man had grown. Humans, indeed!

"That's it!" He uncurled and recurled his toes with a brisk snap. "The wolf. I've got to take care of the wolf. Without the wolf, they're helpless."

Roxanne shuddered. "What are you talking about, Teddy?"

"I'll kill the wolf. I have enough elixir to take care of him."

"You can't kill the white wolf, Teddy."

"Who says I can't?"

"What will Mother Nature say? She'll be furious, Teddy. You can't do this."

He grunted at the mention of the platinum blonde who had so clearly failed to understand his mission. Mother Nature, indeed!

"I can do it. I will do it. And when I have control of Toyland, I will demonstrate to that bubble-headed Mother Nature and everyone else in the world that it's not nice to fool Uncle Teddy!"

Chapter Eleven

Nothing to dread . . .

All day long, Nick had felt the strangest things were happening.

First there had been the strange malaise that had so suddenly come over the white wolf.

One moment the powerful beast had been trotting along beside them, grinning into the wind, and the next he had simply fallen to the ground as if struck by a bullet.

With a cry of alarm, they had both knelt beside the animal, who looked up at them with empty, glazed eyes. The eyes of death. Nick felt his nose; it was hot and dry. His hand over the animal's muzzle detected no sign of breath. He spread his palm on the animal's broad rib cage, checking the heartbeat. He found none.

"What is it, Nick?" Virginia's voice held the crackling beginnings of panic.

"I'm . . . I don't know. If . . . if I didn't know better . . ."

"What?" Virginia demanded impatiently, her hand trembling over the wolf's regal head.

"He's... Virginia, he's dead."

"No!" Virginia shouted. "No! I won't let him be! He can't be!"

And she gathered the massive beast into her lap, cradling his head against her narrow chest as if the mere fact of her closeness could protect him. Tears glimmered in her eyes as she stared defiantly up at Nick. "I'm telling you, I won't let anything happen to him!"

She held him, crooned to him in the soft, low voice that women had known for centuries, rocked him, soothing his brow with a rhythmic stroke. Even where he stood, some feet away, Nick felt the strength of the comfort emanating from her.

But, of course, it was pointless. There was no sign of life in the animal.

Then it happened. The sky flashed brightly. Almost like lightning, but without the sharp intensity. And with a mellow, rolling growl from deep in its throat, the white wolf leapt to his feet.

Neither Nick nor Virginia spoke for the longest time. They simply stared at the animal and then at each other.

"You were wrong," Virginia said softly at last.

Nick said nothing.

Yes, he was growing accustomed to strange things.

In fact, he had even accustomed himself to the fact that the past few days had wrought some strange transformation within him. When he looked at Virginia, heard her laughter, felt the warmth of her hand in his, he felt whole and unscathed in a way he had never felt before.

But the transformation of the Arctic, a change he could see with his own eyes—that he was not willing to accept quite so easily.

The boundary of the North Pole, the Akuchti had told him, was marked by an unusual ice formation. The ice had grown up in a ring, a series of stalagmites rising up from the ground, two to three feet high. A barrier, almost as if to prohibit crossing.

But now that he stood along the southern side of that ridge of ice, he realized Tom Elkhorn had been holding out on him. Tom hadn't told him the strangest thing of all.

North of that boundary, the North Pole was no longer an Arctic wasteland.

Just across the border, sparse tufts of evergreen vegetation dotted the white terrain. Then, as his eyes wandered deeper into the land across the boundary, he saw towering fir trees and plump holly bushes.

"That doesn't even look like ice anymore, Nick," Virginia said, edging closer to the boundary. "It looks like snow."

Soft, powdery snow.

"Is this as weird as I think it is?" She turned to him for confirmation.

He avoided looking her directly in the eyes. "Weird? Well, um, yes. Somewhat. 'Weird' is probably exactly the right word."

He registered the fact that neither he nor the usually unrestrained Virginia had scrambled across the boundary upon reaching it. Even the white wolf lay down at the edge of the boundary, alternately studying his two companions and the landscape beyond.

"It's almost like...a Christmas card." Virginia sounded uncharacteristically hesitant. "An old-fashioned, winter-wonderland Christmas card."

"Yes. Well..."

"I guess we should...get going?"

The warnings of the Akuchti—that those who crossed over might not be permitted a return crossing—seemed suddenly no longer incongruous in light of the unlikely scene before him. Nick grabbed Virginia's arm before she could step over the icy barrier.

"Wait."

She turned to look at him.

"If you cross over..." He stumbled over the words she needed to hear.

"Tell me, Nick."

"The Akuchti say you can't return."

"Well, that's..." She turned her gaze back to the picturesque terrain; when she continued, her voice sounded uncertain once again. "...silly?"

"They say once you cross over, your life is at the mercy of the...magic."

"Magic?"

He drew a deep breath and nodded.

"Nick, you don't look like a man who believes in fairy tales."

He heard in her voice a desperation to hold on to her reporter's skepticism. "If I've learned one thing in my travels, it's never to belittle the wisdom of the locals."

"This isn't local wisdom, Nick. This is superstition."

"Superstition? Maybe." He looked down at the white wolf, then back at Virginia. Her gaze retraced the path his eyes had taken, and he saw she understood. The white wolf was only superstition, too. "What it really comes down to, Virginia, is this—do you believe in what you've come all this way to find?"

"Are you asking me if I believe in Santa Claus, Nick?"

Her direct question didn't make him feel as foolish as he had expected. "I'm asking if you believe in your mission. A mission that's a lot more complex than believing in Santa Claus." As he spoke, Nick felt his passion growing for the words tumbling out of him. "Do you believe in dreams, Virginia? Do you believe in hope? Do you believe children have a right to expect a few years of uncomplicated happiness before reality intrudes?"

He saw tears spring to her eyes and wasn't surprised when she turned away. But he was too caught up in the surprising depth of his own emotions to be stopped by her hurtful memories.

"Do you, Virginia? Because if you don't, you shouldn't cross over."

She whirled on him once again, and he saw that her momentary mistiness had been replaced with her usual hardheaded determination.

"I believe in deadlines, Nick. I believe in doing the job you set out to do. Believing in dreams is not part of the job description. Objectivity is."

When she started to turn toward the North Pole, he grasped her in an unyielding grip, forcing her to give in to his searching gaze. And when he at last saw something beneath the tough professionalism she was determined to project, he released her.

She crossed over. And without a second thought, Nick crossed over, as well.

They stood in silence within the ridge of ice that circled the North Pole. Power—a force that was gentle in its quiet strength—began to seep through Nick, filling him from below, beginning with his toes, flowing upward, surging through his legs and chest and head, pulling him skyward. He wanted to reach for Virginia, make sure this feeling passed from him to her. But before he could find the ability to move, she spoke in a reverent whisper.

"Do you feel it?"

Their hands met and clasped without any conscious movement.

"What is it?" she asked.

The answers seemed to swirl through the air between them, and there was no need to speak them aloud. And as the many improbable notions whirled around them, the intensity of the moment gradually passed.

Virginia laughed, a breathless little sound. "Well. Maybe the Akuchti were right."

And although he heard the attempt at humor in her voice, the look they exchanged was not one of amusement. Nor was it one of disbelief. Nick didn't know how to describe it, except that they seemed to understand something they couldn't quite put meaning to.

As they hoisted their backpacks into position again, Virginia turned to beckon the white wolf, who had not followed them across the pole's boundary.

"Come on, pal. We're ready to roll."

He simply stared.

No matter how much she cajoled, the giant wolf who had been their companion for the past week wouldn't come any closer. Virginia turned woeful eyes on Nick.

"What are we going to do?"

Nick looked from her to the animal. "I think he feels his job is over."

"But he's our friend. And we need him. To protect us. Don't we?"

Nick shrugged. "If Tom Elkhorn was right, we're safe now."

Virginia looked uncertain. "We're still in the middle of the Arctic. We saw a polar bear the size of King Kong not three hours ago. He's probably got his binoculars trained on us right now. How can you think we're safe?"

"The Akuchti have been right up till now, haven't they?"

"I think the wolf should come with us."

Nick let his pack slide back to the ground and squatted to perch on it. "Okay. You go get him."

"All right. I will."

And she stalked to the border, right up to the edge that separated the ice-encrusted tundra from the fluffy, ankle-high drifts north of the boundary. Then she stopped. Abruptly. Increasingly comfortable with the idea that there were forces at work he couldn't control or understand, Nick watched without surprise.

Virginia simply stood and stared across the perfectly unformidable barrier at the silver-eyed animal. She seemed to tremble, as if swaying in the wake of hurricane-force winds. Nick knew what was coming when she turned back to him, her face forlorn.

"I...can't."

"I know."

She walked to him slowly, looking uncertain. He stood as she reached him and took her in his arms. She quivered there; he felt her fear in the face of something she couldn't understand.

He almost hoped she hadn't noticed that the moment they touched, the sky brightened, turned a soft shade of violet along the horizon, almost as if the sun were ready to rise. Yet another reversal of the laws of nature might be too much for one day.

"What's happening to us, Nick? What did I get us into?"

He murmured against her hair, "I don't know, Virginia. All I know is, we're supposed to be here. We're expected. Something in nature wants us here."

She shuddered. "I'm not sure there's anything natural about any of this."

Nick merely held her, hoping she would absorb some of his growing confidence that the magic touching their lives was much more natural than anything man had wrought in the world they had just left.

THWARTED! Theodore hated being thwarted. He had realized, as soon as he felt the strength of the woman's love pulsing through the white wolf, that he didn't have enough elixir to take care of the accursed animal and further his own plans. So he had been forced to trail along behind, keeping his powers off the mangy beast.

But as soon as he was in charge, the overgrown mutt would be the first to go.

For the time being, he would give this business of stopping the human couple one more shot. Then, regardless of what happened, he would turn his efforts to the coup. A simple infiltration of Toyland Compound, the judicious overdose of Elfin Elixir to pump himself up, and he would be too powerful for anyone to stop.

Especially these pitiful humans who didn't even understand the power now at their disposal.

He followed them. At close range. It was easy now that they had left the tundra and wandered deeper into the forest skirting the compound. They were on an unerring path to the compound entrance.

But they wouldn't make it.

He watched as they walked and talked and touched. They shed a layer of their clothes as the climate near the compound moderated. They laughed.

At times the emotion between them was almost strong enough to overpower Theodore's Elfin Elixir. The elixir wasn't meant to work in opposition to this foolish feeling; it was designed, he knew, to grow more potent when used in conjunction with these human emotions. Kris had taught him that.

But Theodore was confident. His control was superior. Destiny was on his side. Besides, he was also picking up another emotion—the woman's fear.

Her fear had surfaced the instant she realized she couldn't cross back into the tundra. It had seized her, shooting through Theodore with toe-straightening intensity. His very skin had glowed white-hot for seconds as she grappled with her terror.

Theodore's empathetic sensations had dimmed somewhat when the man took her in his arms. But there was enough fear still coursing through her to keep him properly energized. Even the man had a small measure of fear skittering around the edges of his mental calm.

Theodore could take them. He knew it. Felt it. Gloried in it.

Abruptly, it seemed to Theodore, they stopped. He landed noiselessly in a pine tree above them. They had reached the skate pond. It glittered in the sunshine. How many carefree January nights had he and the other elves partied around this pond? Theodore's pulse beat more quickly as he realized how close to home he was, how close to achieving everything he'd ever wanted.

"Nick, am I nuts or is the sun shining?" she asked, her soft voice floating up to Theodore. He hated to admit it, but she was almost appealing.

"I think we're both nuts."

She nodded. "That's the only answer."

They dropped their packs and began rummaging through them.

"Nick, if I don't eat something besides salami and jerky soon, I'm going to make a salad out of one of these pine trees."

"How about fish?"

She laughed. It was a musical sound that almost disarmed Theodore. He sniffed around for her fear to boost his immunity. It was weak, but he did the best he could with it.

"Fish. Sure. Why don't you grill us a couple of salmon steaks, Closthaler?"

"Okay."

Theodore sprang to alertness as the man led the woman onto the ice-covered pond. Choosing his spot carefully, the man prepared for ice fishing, explaining his method at every step.

He cut the ice carefully, gauging the depth, taking care not to weaken the surrounding surface. He fashioned a pole from a nearby fallen limb and pulled out the synthetic rope coiled at his waist to fashion a line. They settled around the hole in the ice to wait.

Theodore waited, too.

He ignored the cheerful sounds of their chatting. He mustered his powers, focusing his energies on the few remaining shards of uneasiness in the two humans. He fed on the fear, letting it blossom and grow in him. It quickened his heartbeat, heightened the buzz of energy flowing from brain to toe. Then, when he felt the power raging through him, he opened his eyes and zeroed in on the humans. Waiting for his moment.

It came when the woman decided something nibbled at her pole. With a gleeful shriek, she leaned over the opening in the ice. Leaned just a trifle too far, a trifle too enthusiastically. And with every ounce of power he could muster, Theodore gave her a mental push.

She crashed through the ice.

Chapter Twelve

Visions of sugarplums...

Virginia's headfirst plunge into the icy water took her breath away. She gulped instinctively, flooding her lungs.

She ordered herself to remain calm. Instead, she flailed. Struggling to float, she felt the weight of her sodden clothes dragging down her arms, her legs.

Not ready to die, her mind screamed at her.

She sank anyway. Her lungs ached for oxygen. Determined not to give in, she groped for the surface, her movements sluggish. The shadowy circle of light in the center of the eerie darkness was far above her. Too far.

She wished for one stark moment that she had stayed with the Vanosdal family in Hastings long enough to finish those summer swimming lessons.

She wished in a second stark moment that she hadn't put off telling Nick just how much she had come to love him.

Even though he was terrified of water.

Her third wish—and three was all you were ever granted, wasn't it?—was that there really was a Santa Claus. Because if there was, she had just one thing on her list for this Christmas.

How about a lifeline, Mr. Claus?

Her lungs were bursting. Her eyes saw only darkness.

TERROR GRABBED Nick by the throat.

He couldn't breathe. He couldn't move. He couldn't even think.

All he could do was feel. First the agony of seeing Virginia's golden head plunge beneath the icy water. And then, in the split second that followed, the panicky realization that only he could save her.

And he could no more jump in the water after her than he could fly.

Perspiration broke out on his forehead, his back, his chest. He gulped air, the only way he could seem to breathe.

Virginia, drowning.

Him, letting her. Because nobody knew better than Nick Closthaler just how much the water terrified him.

You can save her. If you believe enough, said an inner voice.

Nick decided it was time he learned to believe.

VIRGINIA HEARD a high, lilting sound, a sound that rose above all the water-muffled sounds around her. Like the jingling of a bell.

Then she felt the lifeline in her hand.

More than a lifeline. An arm. A big, solid arm. It wrapped itself around her waist. Then she was floating up, toward the tiny circle of light she could no longer see.

When the top of her head burst through the surface of the water into the air, into the startling sunlight, she almost gave in to the unconsciousness tugging at her waterlogged brain.

Instead, her eyes flew open, and she looked into Nick's worried, dripping face.

Gasping, she filled her lungs with air. She clung to Nick's chest as they bobbed in the narrow opening in the ice.

"I thought...you couldn't...swim," she gasped out.

"I can't."

"But..."

His eyes were filled with the kind of wonder she had never seen in the eyes of a full-grown man. He smiled gently. "When are you going to realize, Virginia, there is no explanation for any of this?"

As she clung to his solid form for one more sweet moment, she heard a shrill wailing overhead, as if some woodland creature native to this unnatural part of the Arctic were in mourning.

In light of the joy in her soul, the sound was as incongruous as everything else that had happened to her since the moment she met Nick Closthaler.

THEIR CLOTHES HUNG from small shrubs, drying in the muted sunshine they had not yet come to take for granted.

They lay together beneath a blanket on a bed of moss in the shelter of a glade so cozy, so tucked away it might have been fashioned just for them.

"You saved my life," she murmured, warming her cheek against the soft curls scattered over his chest.

"You *are* my life," he murmured in return, his words warming her more deeply even than their intertwined bodies.

"You could've died, too," she protested, lacing one leg around his and drawing her belly against the dark heat of his maleness.

"Without you..."

He didn't finish. He didn't need to; she felt the rest of his thought as vividly as if he continued speaking.

"When I thought I was dying, I thought of you," she whispered. "I was sorry I hadn't told you... that I love you. So I want to tell you now. I love you more than anything."

He swelled against her.

"And I love you. It's so strong, it fills me up."

He began to show her then. He covered her lips with his. She melted against their softness, their possession. She opened to the insistent mating of his tongue with hers; his mouth was sweet with the cool, fresh taste of the outdoors.

The hand beneath her head cradled her tenderly, tangling in her still-damp hair, raising ripples along the back of her neck. His free hand trailed along her back, picking up at the base of her neck where the other left off, teasing its way along the curve of her spine and cupping her buttocks. That hand pulled her closer to feel the heat and steel that rose from him, then it angled between her thighs to caress the heat that rose from her.

She sighed into their kiss and strained into his caress. Her breasts swelled and ached against him. He deepened his touch, seeking softly.

"Fill me, too," she whispered against his lips.

He groaned and nudged his way between her legs. Capturing her eyes with his, he moved into her slowly. He paused to allow them to appreciate their oneness.

She tightened around him. They moved together, and the motion scurried over her, through her, around her.

They moved, slowly and forever. Until the rippling motions overtook her. She cried out again and again.

Then they lay still, clasped together as tightly as possible, refusing to relinquish their joining. She looked into his eyes and saw the magic in them.

"Thank you for saving me," she said.

And she knew she needn't explain that he had saved her from far more than icy water and darkness.

"We've saved each other," he answered.

VIRGINIA STOOD on tiptoe and tried to surreptitiously peer at the compass Nick held in his hands.

"Another half day at most," he pronounced.

Virginia's heart fluttered. A half day from finding out the truth about one of the world's favorite legends! "Do you think we'll find him?"

Nick's look was strange; she understood. She felt strange even asking the question.

"I think we'll find what we came for," he said as they continued trudging through the snow.

She decided not to address his ambiguous answer. Instead, she decided to let her fantasies run wild for a moment. Visions of sugarplums and all that jazz. After all, it was three days before Christmas. Wasn't that what Santa Claus was all about? "What do you want, if you meet Santa?"

He didn't have a ready answer. She glanced over to see his brow knit in concentration as he delved for a reply. Then he looked up and saw her studying him and banished the serious expression. He flashed her a teasing smile.

"A soft bed in a heated room, for a change."

She laughed and thumped him on the arm. "Actually that would be nice. What else?"

"What would you ask for?"

"Before or after the hot shower? How about..." She groped for a silly or extravagant answer. But the only thing that came to mind was neither. And as much as she hated to jinx the thought by voicing it, she couldn't resist.

"A family," she said on a wistful sigh. "A mommy—that's me—and a daddy—that's you—and about six little Clost-Holleys running around playing Nintendo and reading *Green Eggs and Ham.*"

He nodded thoughtfully.

"Doesn't that sound good to you?" she asked, trying not to let his silence alarm her.

"Of course." Then, as if sensing her apprehension, he stopped and took her in his arms briefly. "It does. Better than anything I can imagine."

She heard the "but" in his voice and wasn't certain, as they continued their march across the snowy landscape, how to coax him to open up. She decided that would come with time and let her mind trip along to the next of the many thoughts filling her head.

"Will we have to walk all the way back across the tundra, Nick? If there is a Santa, maybe Rudolph and the boys will fly us back. I'm really eager to get home."

Again, silence.

"Aren't you? Back to Colorado? Start our new life together?"

He spoke as if the reluctant words were coaxed out of him against his will. "Virginia, I'm not sure it's going to be that simple."

"What are you talking about?"

"I'm not sure...no, that's not true. I am sure. I'm sure I won't be going back to Colorado."

She felt herself tense, told herself not to jump to conclusions. Nick was not yanking her dream out from under her yet. Not this quick, for goodness' sake. She tried to keep her voice light. "You're not making much sense, Closthaler."

"This is where I belong."

"Here?" She knew her voice edged toward shrillness, but she couldn't help it. "You want to stay *here?*"

"I was brought here for a reason. I'm going to stay."

"Stay? Nick, you can't mean that. That's the craziest thing I've ever heard. You're... It's a joke, right? You're yanking my ankle, right?"

"No, Virginia. It's not a joke."

And she saw from the implacable determination in his eyes that he definitely was not joking. The cold had gotten to him. Icy water from the pond when he saved her had seeped into his ears and frozen the part of his brain that regulated his sanity. Reason was going to have to prevail, she told herself. And it clearly would not be forthcoming from Nick.

She spoke calmly, as one would speak to a child. "Nick, there aren't a lot of salaried positions up here."

"I manage to get by in Sugarplum Bluff."

He was serious. Lord help them, he thought this made perfect sense. "Okay, then. What about the children in Sugarplum Bluff? Who'll see about them next year when the holiday rolls around?"

He smiled, a secret smile unlike any of his other smiles. "I'm sure when the time comes I'll have the answer for that."

He meant it. All the euphoric contentment she had begun to allow herself to feel these past few days with Nick was about to come crashing down around her ears. It was a sound she should be used to by now. Nevertheless, she felt a lump in her throat and reminded herself once again that reporters don't cry. She growled instead. "Nick, don't spoil this for me."

"Spoil it? What are you talking about?"

"I'm about to break one of the world's biggest news stories. This should be a moment of triumph for me." She fought to keep her voice from trembling. "I've found the man I want to spend my life with. I can actually envision being a family for the first time in my life. I will not allow you to go off the deep end and..."

Nick put a hand on hers. His voice was gentle but firm. "The world's biggest news story? Is that all you see here?"

"Are you listening to me? I also said you're the man I want to spend my life with, make a family with. And I—"

"This is bigger than us, Virginia. Bigger than two people in love. And it's a hell of a lot bigger than headlines and professional acclaim."

"Bigger than us?" She felt as if she'd been slapped. Catching her breath was next to impossible. "Bigger than our love? This stupid trek through the ice and snow is bigger than our love?"

She saw the hurt in his eyes and felt no remorse. His hurt was no match for the betrayal she felt in her heart at this moment.

"Is that what you're saying, Nick?"

"Yes, Virginia. That's exactly what I'm saying."

ELSA, OF COURSE, was so distraught she immediately ate four gingerbread people.

Kris, to be sure, had little enthusiasm for calming her—and even less time.

"Elsa," he said sternly, pushing her into a kitchen chair and frowning as imposingly as his plump red cheeks and cherrylike nose permitted. "We have no time for hysteria. It is December 22. I have work to do. If there is a problem, we will worry about it on December 26."

He was pleased to see that his wife, who had indeed been a stalwart companion and helper at all times, squared her shoulders, cleared her eyes of all hint of dismay and brushed the gingerbread crumbs from her bosom.

"You're right, Kris. We have work to do." Her voice quavered only slightly. "Plenty of time to worry about that foolish young couple and their squabbling after the journey."

With a firm shake of her head, she stood and bustled away in the direction of the stuffed-toy division, which was always behind and seemed to respond only to Elsa's gentle persuasion.

On aching feet, one crisis averted, Kris hobbled back to his office, where Noel was hunched over the computer screen.

"How's it coming?"

Noel shook his head. "Well, the turbo will definitely work. Still bugs, of course. Kinks to work out. In an ideal world, I wouldn't take it out yet. Another year to work on it and—"

"We may not have another year, Noel. The turbosleigh may be our only shot. And after all this time, Theodore can't have much elixir left, if any. With the turbo, we could easily lose him." Kris noted that Noel's nod was anything but reassuring. "How about security? Any talk of this floating about?"

"Hard to tell, Kris. There's something..."

"A leak?"

"Maybe." He was hedging.

"What, Noel?"

"The tank—" He hesitated.

"The elixir?"

Noel nodded. "The lock's been jimmied."

Kris gasped. "Missing elixir?"

"Not yet. The lock held. We've stepped up security."

"Someone working for Theodore."

"Maybe."

"Maybe? What in holy holly berries does 'maybe' mean?"

Noel's voice was irritatingly placating. "Well, boss, we really don't have any indication there are any Theodore loyalists in the compound."

"Then who?"

"We think he's back."

"Teddy?" Kris sank into his chair. "In the compound?"

"Afraid so, boss. Radar showed a break in the psych ring around the compound sometime last night. And we found faint traces of green dust in the woods outside the compound."

"Green dust," Kris muttered. "Only a very sick elf sheds green dust."

Noel nodded.

With a decisive clap of his hands, Kris sprang to his feet. "Go after the humans, Noel. We don't have time to waste. And we can't risk any more unexpected disasters. If Theodore does manage to get his hands on any more elixir..."

Neither of them could bear to put into words the images that fluttered through their minds.

THEODORE FELT more relaxed now that he was actually breathing Toyland Compound air, filled as it was with the potent helium expelled each time the thousands of elves in the region breathed out.

He was also happy to be sitting in the familiar comfort of the secret underground tunnel Roxanne had maintained in his absence. After his ouster, the elves had closed it up, but it had been an easy matter—a tweak of the toes here, a flick of the ear there, Roxanne had assured him—to shift the earth again and restore the homey comfort to the dark, dank hole in the ground.

Here was his favorite chair, a big, puffy affair that he could curl up in like a kitten. His footstool. Even the pair of gold-and-teal brocade slippers he had left behind in his hastily arranged departure.

At last something had gone right.

The bungled drowning had undermined his confidence and nearly depleted his supply of Elfin Elixir. And Roxanne's ineptitude the night before in breaking into the hold where the stuff was stored had been a grave disappointment.

But here, surrounded by the comfort of the familiar, he knew triumph was inevitable. And close at hand.

"I think bribery will work," he mused.

Roxanne shook her head. "Only the most loyal are allowed to guard the elixir right now, Teddy. The old man knows something is up."

He hated it when Roxanne was right.

"Then you must use your feminine wiles, Roxie."

Roxanne looked down at her plump figure, which was somewhat the worse for wear thanks to the difficult weeks of travel. "Huh?"

"Seduce someone, Roxanne. Or hit them over the head. But I have every confidence you can take care of it."

"Why do I always get stuck with the dirty work?"

All his anger and frustration of the past two weeks—no, the past two years, since his exile—bubbled to the surface. Theodore whirled on her, eyes glowing and green dust flying in all directions.

"You are just following orders, Roxanne," he hissed. "That's all you need to remember. I am putting every bit of energy I have into making this world a better place and I don't need second-guessing from you."

She withered. "Okay. Okay. Sorry, Teddy. You're right. I'll get the elixir."

He drew a deep, slow breath, drawing plenty of helium into his lungs. "Good. I'll need enough to take over the reindeer team tomorrow night."

Still shaking, she nodded. "Gotcha."

"Oh, and one more thing. I'll need enough to send that cute little human couple right back to Colorado."

"That's no trouble, Teddy. We'll put them on the sleigh right after the journey and—"

"No, no, no. That's not good enough. I want to send them back about—" he paused to calculate "—about four weeks. Back to a time before they met."

The glow returned to his eyes; he felt it burning up from his gullet. "That's what I'll do. Banish them both. And make sure they never cross paths again."

Chapter Thirteen

A bundle of toys
he had flung on his back....

Virginia's enthusiasm for one of the world's biggest news stories fizzled as the tension between her and Nick crackled.

She glared at him—rather at his back, as he stalked ahead of her—for the first hour after he callously informed her that her dream of belonging to a family, of having people who would love her forever and ever no matter what, had once again been snatched beyond her reach.

Now they sat under opposite trees in a clearing and ate—actually Virginia pretended to eat; she had no appetite and couldn't swallow even if she had. She could hardly look at him.

His broad, capable hands hurt her heart. His shoulders, his silvering hair, the distinguished pewter-colored beard that was growing fuller every day—all of it hurt. What upset her most of all, however, were his eyes. Because they revealed no pain whatsoever. They were completely and inarguably serene.

The rift between them didn't even bother him.

How could she have been so wrong about what had happened between them? How could she have felt so much, when he obviously felt so little? How had her usually right-on instincts failed her so miserably?

"I'm glad your appetite isn't suffering," she snapped, then was angry with herself for letting her emotions show.

Even his voice was serene, darn his hide. "It's going to work out, Virginia."

"Of course it is. I'm going to file my story and win a Pulitzer Prize and get hired by the *Washington Post* and cover the White House the rest of my life, and you're going to live up here with polar bears, eat beef jerky and moon-bathe in your thermal underwear six months out of the year!" Her voice rose with each word. "How delightful! It's going to work out fine! Of course it is!"

He almost smiled. She would swear to it. Just a twitch at the corner of his mouth. As if he could see some warped humor in their situation but knew she was not yet in the mood to joke about it.

She almost threw her sausage roll at him.

"His noggin's so hard, he probably wouldn't feel a thing anyway," came the high-pitched tones of a commiserating voice from her left.

Jumping at the sound, Virginia almost slipped off the stump where she perched. When she righted herself, she looked around to see a tiny, gaily dressed—person?—lounging under a tree, gazing from her to Nick and back again with piercing eyes that were a most unusual shade of topaz.

"Well, he is hardheaded, wouldn't you say?" The little creature with the squeaky voice smiled at her. "A sausage roll would hardly do any damage at all, that's my guess."

Virginia knew her mouth was open, but she couldn't seem to do a thing about it. All she could do was stare at the—person?—in the bright green tunic, opaque red tights and pointy-toed slippers.

"I'm hallucinating," she said at last, turning to Nick. "You don't see what I see, do you? It's me. My brain is frostbitten and I'm hallucinating."

Nick looked toward the tree where Virginia's mirage lounged. "Looks like an elf to me."

Virginia groaned. "Oh, lord, we've both lost our grip on reality."

The creature jumped up and, in one arcing leap, landed feather light in the clearing between them. "Oh, no. I'm quite real. Most assuredly real."

Virginia looked up and captured Nick's eye, then mouthed silently, "Grab him."

Then he made another unannounced and geophysically improbable leap and returned to the relative safety of the tree on the other side of the clearing. When Nick made no move to nab this apparently real, live creature, Virginia knew it was up to her.

She lunged.

Her aim was good. She had him by the waist, both arms solidly anchored around his waifish frame. There was something primitively satisfying in feeling so massive, so powerful—downright macho, she thought with relish—next to such an impish individual. But before she could enjoy the unprecedented sensation of being at least a comparative amazon, he disappeared.

Slithered right out of her grip. Like air.

Pulling herself up off the ground, Virginia looked around frantically. He now perched on a holly bush near Nick.

"No need to panic, Virginia. I'm not going anywhere. At least, not without you two. I've come for you, you see."

Brushing the twigs from her knees, she challenged the slippery apparition. "How did you know my name?"

He smiled. "Oh, we all know your name by now."

"Who's 'we'?"

The little man looked at Nick. "Does she always ask so many questions?"

Nick smiled. "She's a newspaper reporter."

The little man's faceted eyes transformed to amethyst, and he studied Virginia more closely. "Oh, my. I thought reporters were all...seedy types. With big hats and trench coats and cigars. I guess I've watched *Miracle on Thirty-fourth Street* too many times. But I do love the part where they bring in all the bags of mail and..."

"Who are you?" Virginia made her stance and her voice as imposing as possible and wondered if she could somehow edge closer and take this little person by surprise.

"Yes. Well, I suppose I should begin at the beginning. Although it would be nice if you would agree to come along without asking so many questions." He looked at Virginia, then shook his head. "No, I guess not. Well, I'm Noel."

He paused as if that should mean something and looked disappointed when Virginia didn't react.

"I'm Kris's chief assistant."

"Kris who?"

"Kris Kringle, of course."

"Kris Kringle." She rolled her eyes at Nick; he was inconsiderate enough to continue regarding their elfin intruder as if all this made perfect sense. "As in Santa Claus, I presume?"

"Well, yes, if you prefer. We've simply known him as Kris for centuries. But Santa Claus is fine. Anyway, I'm his chief assistant. And he sent me to bring you straightaway to the Toyland Compound. So, if we could begin ... ?"

And he stood, as if no other explanation should be necessary.

Nick stood, too, and shrugged into his backpack.

"You aren't buying this, are you?" she asked him.

"Isn't this why we came here in the first place?"

"Yes, but ..."

"Then we should go with him, shouldn't we?"

"Yes, but..."

She couldn't think of a legitimate protest. All rational reasons had seemed to fly out the window here in this winter wonderland. Throwing up her hands, she retrieved her own pack from the forest floor.

"Fine. Let's go."

Noel smiled. "Wonderful. Now, if you could just stand shoulder to shoulder and boost me up, I think I can save us some time."

Even as Virginia geared up to protest, Nick stepped beside her, then lifted the tiny man to his shoulder. She barely felt his weight as he straddled their shoulders with his funny little feet.

"All right, everyone, could I get you to close your eyes and concentrate on visions of sugarplums?"

"Oh, get real..." Virginia grumbled.

To her surprise, Noel giggled. "Okay. You're right. Not necessary at all. I just thought it would be fun. However, it might be beneficial if you close your eyes. Keeps the wind out, you know."

Reluctantly she closed her eyes. But they opened instantly when she felt herself rising in the air. Sure enough, the ground was now several feet below them and receding steadily. She quickly snapped her eyes closed again and felt herself being swept higher still. Filled with a combination of terror and exhilaration, she held her breath as they headed into the wind. Not daring to look, absorbing only the feel of the wind at her face and the nothingness beneath her dangling feet, she didn't exhale until she felt herself being gently lowered to earth. She had flown! Through unexpected and unconventional means, she had conquered her old fears.

After steadying herself against Nick's broad shoulder, bravely resisting the urge to drop to her knees and embrace the welcome firmness of the ground, she opened her eyes to see an enormous candy-striped gate.

"The Toyland Compound," Noel pronounced, jumping off their shoulders and pointing at the gate with one of his spindly little fingers.

The gate opened obligingly.

Noel scampered in. Nick took a step in that direction. But Virginia wasn't sure she was ready for what waited beyond. Then Nick turned, smiled and put out his hand.

"I told you, it's going to be fine."

Patting the bulk of her portable computer to anchor herself to something real, Virginia stared at the hand he offered.

"Is that a promise?"

"Yes, as a matter of fact. It is."

She looked into his eyes and saw too many things reflected there to doubt him. The shadows of their lovemaking. The echoes of their conversations. She believed him, despite how betrayed she had felt just minutes earlier.

Swallowing her anxiety, she took his hand and walked through the gate with him. But the minute she stepped inside, she decided it was time to turn and run.

Too late. The gate slid swiftly and silently closed behind them.

"Oh, my gosh," she said in a breathless whisper, "I've landed in Disney World North."

She dropped Nick's hand and turned around to stare in all directions.

Huge, brightly colored buildings stretched and towered in every direction. Red and pink and purple, they seemed to be made of gumdrops and candy canes and gingerbread. Signs over each building looked as if they were written in icing and indicated the activity in each building: Doll Factory; Stuffed Animal Production. The heady aroma of peppermint and chocolate revealed the location of candy manufacturing. As far as Virginia could see, a children's fantasy land stretched before her.

"This is a joke, right?" But even as she said it, she was pulling her notebook out of the side pocket of her backpack and beginning to scribble furiously.

Ozzie would think she'd flipped.

Maybe she had.

She wondered fleetingly if she could get her hands on a camera. Photos to back up her story were going to be a must.

Noel turned to her. "A joke? Oh, my, no. This is serious business. Let me assure you. Deadline pressure, you know."

"Deadline?"

Noel pointed to a giant clock in the center of the courtyard where they stood. The timepiece listed not only the hour, but the date.

"Absolutely. December 23, you see. We're running out of time. And we've never disappointed anyone yet. Don't plan to start this year." She noted the troubled expression that flickered across his face. "No, sir. Not even this year."

Her reporter's instincts sniffed the story in his comment. Pen poised over her notebook, she asked, "But there is trouble in Toyland?"

Nick and Noel exchanged glances.

"Why don't I show you both around?"

"Where is Santa?" Virginia followed. "When can I speak with Mr. Claus? Is there any truth to the rumor that he's planning to retire?"

Noel shook his head, and his ears turned a frightful shade of fuchsia. "In due time. First, perhaps you would find it enlightening to get a firsthand look at how we operate here in Toyland."

"There is a Santa, isn't there?" Virginia persisted. "I mean, it's not just some giant hoax, like *The Wizard of Oz*, with you elves doing all the work and—"

"Giant hoax!"

Noel's ears grew absolutely livid now, and she would have sworn the ends of his funny little shoes actually uncurled a couple of inches. She made a note.

"Toyland is no hoax. Christmas is no hoax. Although I must say, I'm beginning to doubt his judgment."

"Whose judgment?"

"The boss's."

"In what way?"

Noel raised his chin and looked at her sternly. "If you must know, you were hand-picked. And I'm beginning to share some of Elsa's doubts."

"Elsa? Who's Elsa?"

At that point, Nick's hand clasped over her mouth. "Maybe it's time to postpone the inquisition, Virginia. If you'll be quiet long enough to let our friend here conduct his tour, you might get some of the answers you're after."

Emitting an eloquent harrumph, Noel nodded curtly and pointed them toward the doll factory.

The giant pink-and-white building was abuzz. Thousands of tiny people, all dressed like Noel and bearing the same distinctive features of face and ear and toe that Noel bore, worked diligently. Threading tufts of sunshine yellow hair into tiny plastic heads; painting the bloom on thousands of tiny plastic and porcelain cheeks; popping heads and arms and legs into place and double-checking for mobility; sorting through miniature baby rompers and the teensiest of sequined ballgowns.

Every doll that had ever been coveted by a little girl on the planet Earth marched through this enormous room in various stages of creation.

"As you see, doll central still does a booming business. Three million, nine hundred and twenty-two thousand, I believe, this year alone."

Virginia knew she should capture the number in her notes, but all she could do was stare, mouth open.

It was the same throughout the compound. Toy trucks and electronic games and even good old-fashioned jigsaw puzzles. All were being manufactured and packaged and inventoried in unfathomable numbers, then placed on shiny red conveyer belts and zipped right out of the humming factories.

"Where are they going?" Virginia asked.

"Why, distribution central, of course."

"Of course."

"Follow me."

And they followed him out of the building, then around to the back, where all the shiny, speeding conveyer belts snaked and twisted like so many California freeways all converging on the same spot. Virginia felt herself once again losing her grip.

Then Nick took her hand in his. "Hang on, Virginia. It's going to be all right."

She felt her anxiety ebb. But all she could do was look up at him and nod.

Following the convoluted trail, the trio eventually came upon another building. Inside this one, the multitude of conveyer belts converged. And at their end stood a brown canvas bundle, about the size of a college student's laundry bag.

Into its open mouth dropped a game of building blocks. Then a gilt-edged book of fairy tales tipped and tumbled. A stuffed critter fashioned after the latest animated movie rage. A chemistry set. Computer software. A shiny red fire engine. On and on, the toys slipped over the edge into the bundle, which never grew any larger, which never grew misshapen or bulged at the seams. The toys simply seemed to vanish.

"Where are—" Virginia stepped forward, prepared to grab the edge of the bag that was swallowing all the toys when Noel placed a restraining hand on her arm.

"Oh, please. It wouldn't do to disturb the process."

"Process? What process? This stuff is simply disappearing."

"It's all computerized, you know. And if we get it out of whack now, well..." Noel pointed to the oversize face of his wristwatch. "Believe me, in due time, everything will be explained. But right now it's important not to disturb the process as we pack Kris's sack."

Growing quickly exasperated with the matter-of-fact way everyone was expecting her to swallow this ridiculous tale, Virginia stalked along behind Noel as he beckoned her and Nick to "one last stop."

"Who's behind this, do you think?" she hissed at Nick.

"Behind it? Behind what?"

"This...this...con job. Is it only a giant practical joke, do you think? Or is it something else? Are we pawns in some weird plan to take over the world by—"

"Virginia." Nick took her hand in his and squeezed. "Is it so hard for you to believe?"

"Believe? Believe in . . . this?"

"In goodness. In giving. In the magic of spreading happiness."

She stopped and stared at him, unmindful of Noel's impatient glance in their direction. "Nick, you're a smart man. A practical man. You've survived jungles and deserts and Arctic snowstorms. You can't be falling for this."

"Just open your heart, Virginia. Go with what you feel."

What she felt was that the entire world had suddenly stepped into a major drug flashback. But she simply clamped her mouth shut and followed Nick, who followed Noel right through the front door of a cozy little cottage. Inside the cottage, a quick left landed the three of them in the midst of a room that was warm with the smells of cinnamon and nutmeg and cookie dough.

A plump little woman who was almost a full head shorter than Virginia looked up without pulling her floury hands out of the cookie dough she worked. Her face sparkled to rosy life as her eyes lit on Virginia and Nick.

"Oh, how wonderful! You've arrived!" She clapped her hands, generating a cloud of flour, then wiped them on her red-and-white gingham apron. "Oh, I do hope everything is all right. You two have made up, haven't you? I mean, that's going to be quite a monkey wrench in the works if you two aren't...that is..."

Noel stepped forward with a loud clearing of his throat. The white-haired woman glanced at him, and her cheeks grew even rosier.

"What I mean is, would you like a cookie?"

And she reached across the table with a tray of fragrant gingerbread cookies. After days of beef jerky and dried fruit, Virginia thought she'd never smelled anything so wonderful in all her life. Her jaw tightened in anticipation of biting into one. Instead of indulging, however, she extended a hand.

"I'm Virginia Holley. And you're...?"

The woman wiped her right hand once more, then took Virginia's. "Elsa. Elsa Kringle. We're so glad you've finally arrived. That storm. And, of course, they think they've been keeping it from me, but I'm well aware that Theodore was no small threat himself."

She exchanged a smugly satisfied look with Noel, who looked both dismayed and caught at the same time.

"Theodore? Who's Theodore?" Virginia poised her pencil over her notepad once again, brushing away a light dusting of flour with the side of her fist.

"Oh, never mind about Theodore now. Now that you're here, I'm sure everything will be just fine. Did you enjoy your tour?"

"Very much," Nick said, smiling warmly as he took two of the cookies she offered.

"Oh, I'm so glad. You know, you are a much more dashing young man than I was able to discern," Elsa said. "So much like Kris when he was your age. Taller, of course. And a bit broader in the shoulder, I must admit. Most of Kris's broadness is located a little lower in the anatomy, I fear. Gracious' sakes, listen to me go on."

Virginia tapped her pencil on her pad. "Elsa Kringle? Can I assume that you're Mrs. Kringle, then?"

Elsa's eyes danced. "You've heard of me? Oh, how lovely. You know, I really don't mind playing second fiddle, as it were. But I suspect, that is, from what I've seen of you... Well, I suppose things change with the times."

"And these cookies you're making. Santa will take them when he makes his rounds tomorrow night?"

"Oh, absolutely. Of course, I am involved in other things than the cookie making. The dolls are my favorite, although Noel does say no one has my touch with the cookies. And product safety. I've become quite the advocate of product safety in recent years."

Virginia felt her knees giving way and was grateful when Nick shoved a chair behind her. She dropped into it and let her notebook fall into her lap.

"So this is it. The North Pole. And you're Mrs. Claus. And this is chief elf." She shook her head. "I've got to get some pictures. Nobody's going to believe this story without some pictures."

"Story?" Elsa looked at Noel, then Nick, alarm in her eyes. "What does she mean?"

"The story I'm going to write. About discovering Santa Claus. By the way, when do I get to meet him? I can't do this second-hand, you know. I'll have to have a personal interview. How did you feel, Mrs. Kringle, when your husband announced his retirement?"

"Story? Oh, gracious' sakes, my dear, you're not going to write a story about this. Oh, no, that just won't be possible."

"Of course it's possible. That's why I'm here."

Then Elsa Kringle surprised her by emitting a lovely tinkling laugh that rattled the wooden spoons in their racks on the walls.

"Why, don't be silly, my dear. You're not here to write a story. You two nice young people are here to be the next Mr. and Mrs. Claus. Haven't you figured that out yet?"

Chapter Fourteen

Away to the window,
they flew like a flash....

Nick felt a little dizzy when he heard the words spoken aloud for the first time. He leaned against the massive wooden table for support and glanced at Virginia.

Her windburned cheeks had gone completely white. She really hadn't guessed. Even so, she, too, obviously knew the truth of Elsa Kringle's words the minute she heard them.

So did Nick. But was he really prepared to believe in that truth? And act on it?

Before either Nick or Virginia could recover enough to respond to Elsa's cheerfully delivered bombshell, the kitchen door opened once again. And another bombshell was delivered. This one short and stout and bewhiskered and dressed in red from head to foot.

"Blast it all, Noel, that computer is logjammed again, and I'm right in the middle of calling up the change of address list and—" The brusque voice halted midgrumble as merry blue eyes lit on the new-comers to the kitchen. "Well, frost my snowman if you haven't arrived! Noel, why didn't someone let me know our guests had arrived?"

Nick felt a bubble of laughter rising in his throat. And something else, too. A ridiculous, throat-clogging sentimentality. As if he had—finally, after searching all his life—come home. With one hand, he reached for Virginia's shoulder and felt her tremble as the vision before them sank into her consciousness, too.

"I think I'll just faint if that's okay with everybody," she whispered.

All eyes turned toward her breathy voice, but Nick knew with one glance that Virginia had absolutely no intention of giving up consciousness at this particular moment. Her eyes were alert and wide; awareness crackled through her.

"Now, now, young lady," the old gent said in his deep, mellow voice. "No need for that. Not as many times as you've sat on my lap."

Nick heard the little bubble of laughter rising from Virginia's chest.

"You're real. There really is a...a..."

"Oh, yes, Virginia. There really is."

And he smiled with well-deserved satisfaction.

"And you really are retiring?"

Kris nodded. "Indubitably. I'm tired and too old. I can't take many more of these midnight runs. You know how it is, my dear. Deadlines. They'll zap all your strength."

Then he took another step in their direction and clapped his hand on Nick's shoulder. Emotion clogged Nick's throat almost instantly, the touch was so fatherly, so warm. The kind of touch he couldn't remember, no matter how far back he stretched his memory.

At the same time, the touch was robust, belying all complaints of tiredness and age. The touch was also electric with a different kind of energy. Nick felt the energy sing through him, fill him, transform him.

He felt, if he closed his eyes and concentrated, as if he could fly.

A good thing, he supposed. It seemed to be part of the job requirement.

The thought didn't even surprise him. He would stay. He'd known it all along, in the back of his mind, as they made this crazy trek. He'd been preparing for it all his life. And now he'd come home to it. It was that simple.

"But you, young man, I can see now you're going to have all the energy it takes for centuries to come."

Virginia stood abruptly. "What you're telling us, it can't be true."

"Oh, but it is, my dear."

"Even if you are Santa—"

"Oh, I can assure you—"

"Nick and I are just...people. We're not... supernatural. Or whatever it is you have to be to—" She turned to Nick. "Listen to me. I'm trying to discuss this logically. I've lost my mind, too. Tell me you're still in command of your faculties, Nick. Promise me you haven't gone off the deep end, too."

All he could do was put his arm around her and hope that, as she had when they crossed into the North Pole together, she would feel the power passing between them once again. He felt her resist the pull of that power, but he held on anyway.

"Why us?" he asked, keeping one arm around Virginia as he turned to Kris Kringle. "She's right. We are only humans."

"Ah, but now you have the power it takes." The merriment in the old man's eyes now faded, replaced by an ancient wisdom Nick had never before seen in anyone's eyes. "You feel it now. That courage to do what others don't have the conviction for. You had it before, even, but you didn't know it."

The words struck a discordant note in Nick. It was some seconds before he realized why: oddly enough he had heard a variation of the same philosophy—and thought he had rejected it—from the father he had grown up despising. In the back of his mind, he wondered now if this belief in one's own power, which had fostered greed and self-aggrandizement in his father, hadn't somehow been reinvented in himself as something better.

When he looked into Kris's eyes, he saw a satisfied smile as the old man nodded almost imperceptibly.

"And I suppose you're going to teach us how to fly in your sleigh and slide down chimneys," Virginia said. "You'll have an intensive training seminar, I suppose, and—"

Elsa clucked her tongue reprovingly. "I told you she was a problem, Kris. Entirely too headstrong. I don't think she believes a word you're saying."

"She believes," Kris announced with kindly confidence. "She just doesn't know it yet."

HAND IN HAND—as much because Virginia felt the need to hold on to something steady as anything else—she and Nick wandered once again through Toyland Compound. Virginia found herself forgetting Nick's earlier betrayal and drawing closer to him.

"Is this real?" she asked, whispering despite the almost musical tinkle of toy-making equipment that filled the crisp, fresh air. "Is any of this real, or have I fallen into a dream?"

Nick reached out to touch the shiny surface of a racing bicycle just off the assembly line. Virginia watched his hands, his fingers strong yet supple, and felt the reverence in his hands for the craftsmanship.

"You know, I haven't seen a bicycle made like this since I was a kid," he said, his voice deep with wonder. "What you see in the stores today, they're all surface shine. But this..."

He took the hand he held and flattened her palm against the front fender. The metal was solid. Firm. And it resonated with something Virginia could only label emotion.

"Feel that, Virginia? There's pride and integrity and love in that bicycle." He turned to her, his eyes shining. "I know that feeling. I get it every time I make a toy for one of my kids. But I've never felt it anywhere else before, except—"

The oddest expression came over his face.

"Except where, Nick?"

Nick was silent for a long time as he once again ran his hand over the sleek lines of the bike. When he spoke, his voice was soft. "Except in the work my . . . my father did. He had that pride. In spite of everything else, he had it. And he . . . I wonder if he didn't teach it to me."

"I wouldn't be a bit surprised." Moisture clouded Virginia's eyes in response to the emotion singing from Nick's face and vibrating through the hand he held against the bike. "I feel it, too, Nick."

Satisfied, he clasped her hand once again. "Then you have your answer, don't you? About whether it's real?"

She blinked rapidly and swallowed against the tears that didn't quite make sense, like everything else that had happened to her since the day she pulled the fax from the North Pole off the machine in the newsroom.

"You think what they say is right, then? That the reason we're here . . . ?"

Still she couldn't put the overwhelming thought into words.

The back of Nick's strong, hard fingers stroked along her cheek. "I do."

"But if it is so, Nick. What about us?" Just as she had when Nick told her he wouldn't be returning to Colorado with her, Virginia felt her dreams of a family, a life like everyone else had, slipping away. "What about the way we feel about each other? What about children? Picket fences? A station wagon?"

"Maybe those things aren't our destiny, Virginia."

She dropped his hand and crossed her arms over her chest, tucking her hands in tightly. "That's the only destiny I want, Nick. The only destiny I've ever wanted. Since I was a kid, Nick. To be normal. It's not fair, Nick."

Nick sighed, and she saw the understanding in his eyes. He knew about childhood longings; she knew that from all he had told her about his own childhood. But she also knew that he had already accepted what was happening to them. And if she were to have him, she must accept, too.

"I'll try," she said. "I'll try, Nick. But I can't promise."

He simply nodded. But his eyes held the light of certainty that she still couldn't quite coax into her own soul.

Unlocking her arms, she took his hand in hers once again, and they continued their mesmerizing tour through bustling Toyland Compound.

She lost him in the woodworking shop, where the finishing touches were being put on a line of old-fashioned block trains. He stopped one of the elves, a pudgy little fellow with a tip-tilted nose who called himself Wexell, and asked about the hours of hand labor that went into each simple toy. The ensuing conversation captured Nick completely, especially when Wexell invited Nick to take a turn at attaching the movable wheels to one of the cabooses.

Nick looked back at her, questioning and excitement in his eyes, like a little boy seeking permission to dig into all the delights under the twinkling Christmas tree.

She smiled. "You stay here. I've got work of my own to do."

Then she turned back toward the cozy cottage where Kris and Elsa lived, found her backpack, unloaded her portable computer and took it into Kris's office. It was time to file her story.

But when she sat at the desk—the only desk she had ever sat behind that didn't dwarf her; living with elves could have its up side, she supposed—the cursor on her screen blinking back at her, Virginia found it difficult to know where to begin this story that would stun the world when it opened its newspapers on Christmas morning.

North Pole—Calling himself Kris Kringle, the four-hundred-year-old man who is responsible for everything under your tree this morning has been located at a remote...

No. Too stuffy.

North Pole—Santa Claus lives!

No. Too sensational.

North Pole— His eyes, how they twinkle. His dimples, how merry.

No. It's been done.

Virginia sighed and slumped back in her chair, deleting the words on the screen just as the gentleman in question walked into the room. The force of his personality filled the air and seeped into her soul.

"Ah, Virginia. I was hoping to find you here." He patted his belly with satisfaction and crooked a finger at her. "Come here. Got something I think you'll enjoy."

Giving her empty screen one last baleful look, she stood and followed Kris to the other desk in the room. On it sat a small silver box centered on a silver pedestal.

"Here," Kris said, pulling out the chair and gesturing for her to sit. "You do the honors."

"But..."

"Now, now. No arguments, young lady. It's still not too late for me to fill your stocking with a bundle of switches."

And his booming laughter filled the room, beckoning Virginia to join him in the moment of merriment.

"Now, all you do is sit here and wrap your hands around the pedestal," he said as she followed his instructions. "Like so."

The silver was warm against her skin, which surprised her.

"Then I'll boot this thing up—foolish talk, if you ask me, but Noel insists on all this electronic mumbo jumbo—while you sit back and... feel."

The silver box hummed to life. Joy pierced Virginia's heart so suddenly and so poignantly she involuntarily jerked her hands away from the box. The sensation of childlike pleasure receded instantly.

Kris's hands covered hers and led them back to the pedestal. "Not to be afraid now. This is how we stay in touch. And it's become my greatest pleasure, I must tell you."

Apprehensive, she nevertheless let him press her hands back into position. When she did, the sensation of joy flooded her again. Flooded her so completely she felt seven again. Not the way she had felt at seven, but the way she had always believed the other seven-year-olds in the world felt. Innocent and open and overwhelmingly certain that life was filled with magic and goodwill and dreams come true.

Jason. An effervescent, mischievous blond. Excited by the smell of sugar cookies. Captured momentarily by the twinkle of the star atop the tree in the

*living room. How much longer, Mommy? A big hug.
A big, mother's hug. Warm enough to snuggle into.
Soaring joy.*

For the second time that day, Virginia felt tears mist
her eyes and constrict her chest. "What is this?"

Kris's voice was husky with wonder. "My pipeline.
The most precious thing I get from this job."

*Allyson. Can't keep still. Red velvet dress. Jingle
bells on her socks. The Christmas pageant. The first
Noel. Daddy, tell me again. Tell me again how the an-
gels heard on high. Tell me again about baby Jesus.
Big arms. A safe lap. Dozing off. Fighting sleep. Does
everybody love baby Jesus, Daddy?*

Virginia's tears flowed freely now. "I don't understand. It's as if . . . I'm in their skin. Inside their little
hearts. I can feel them."

She heard tears in Kris's voice when he answered.
"That's exactly right, Virginia. This is my direct
pipeline right into the hearts of all my little ones. Listen. Feel."

From all over the world, from millions of little
hearts and minds, Virginia felt the outpouring of love
and excitement and pleasure that is the spirit of the
holiday. She felt the joys of childhood. The children
filled her. Only when Kris took her in his arms and
held her to his ample chest was she able to stop cry-
ing.

"It's almost like they're mine," she said. "My children. My family. The family I never had."

"They will be," Kris said, his voice as soothing as the gentle hand on her head. "Every single one of them."

THAT NIGHT, lying with Virginia's head on his shoulder in the big feather bed in front of the smoldering fireplace in the cozy bedroom Elsa had—reluctantly—assigned them, Nick sensed Virginia's turmoil.

He had found great satisfaction in the hours he had spent working with his hands in one factory after another this afternoon and late into the evening. On the eve of Christmas Eve, the elves had worked at a frenzied pace, but as midnight neared everyone breathed a little more easily. The quotas would be met. No child would go wanting.

Virginia's red-rimmed eyes and uncharacteristic quiet, however, told him she was not as comfortable with the way her afternoon had gone.

He tightened his arm around her narrow shoulders. Her breasts were full and soft against his chest. Her feathery curls tickled his neck. Her scent entered his nostrils and worked its way into his bloodstream, where it began to drum insistently.

"I think Elsa believes we should marry," he said into the darkness made golden around the edges by the dying embers in the fireplace.

Virginia stiffened. "Elsa is old-fashioned."

"So am I."

She was silent for too long. He kissed the top of her head. Her hand sneaked its way into his and begged him to snuggle it protectively into his grasp.

"What happened this afternoon, Virginia?"

Again she was silent, but he felt her gathering her thoughts.

"I don't think I'll be filing a story, Nick."

"I know." He felt her free hand splay itself on his belly. Warmth gathered beneath it, spiraled outward. "Does that mean you're staying?"

His heart picked up its pace as he waited for her answer. This was where he belonged; he had sensed that for days before they even arrived, before he even understood what place this was. But if Virginia didn't stay...

"He let me touch the children today, Nick."

"What children?"

"All the children. All over the world. I touched their hearts, Nick. I thought their thoughts and felt their feelings. They were...mine."

He heard the awe in her voice and let himself relax a little, despite the fact that she had avoided his question, had made no commitment.

"How did it feel, Virginia?"

"Like the greatest love in the world, Nick."

He felt her body glow warmer from the remembered love. "Then how can you not stay?"

"Kris said they would be my family."

"He should know."

"Yes. Still..."

"Still you hesitate."

"Still, he and Elsa have no children of their own. No one they could watch grow up. Read stories to. They've given bicycles to millions, billions of children. And they've never had the pleasure of teaching their own child to ride a bike."

"Maybe they're fulfilled without that. Maybe they have so much..."

"Maybe."

But she wasn't convinced. And he wasn't certain how he could answer.

So he gave her the only comfort he had. He lifted her face to his and kissed her soft, warm lips. He placed all the love he had to share in his kiss, in his touch. And he felt her bloom beneath him, felt her grow pliant and aching and heated. Even as he bloomed and grew rigid and aching and heated.

His kisses, his caresses, followed every womanly swell of hip and breast. He tasted her sweetness. And the sweetest of all was her response—the breathless moans when he drew her nipple into his mouth; the arching invitation when he drew his hand down her belly to find her warmth; the half smile of escalating pleasure when he tickled the inside of her knee with the tip of his tongue.

She responded, too, by returning his love. With her small, soft hands, she smoothed every inch of tense muscle along his back, his belly, his thighs. Her tiny mouth covered his hair-rough body with kisses.

Then she pulled him to her, into her. As they moved together, as their eyes locked, as their sensations came into full bloom, Nick had trouble not saying what was on his mind.

How could this not be enough for anyone?

Instead, he said the only thing he knew with certainty. "I love you, Virginia. With the greatest love *I've* ever known."

With her passion, she answered.

But he couldn't be certain what her answer would be when the heat of passion subsided.

THE FIRST SOUND they heard when they awoke the next morning was a shrill shriek that sounded like an alarm. The sound pierced the pleasant hum of activity that had filled the compound the day before. Both sprang from their bed and flew like a flash to the window.

Tearing open the shutters, they peered out into the courtyard, where Kris and Elsa had just dashed out to join dozens of alarmed-looking elves.

Suddenly the shrill alarm fell silent. And a smug voice filled the air in its place.

"Good morning, boys and girls. This is Theodore. And what a wonderful Christmas Eve surprise I've brought for all my old friends."

Chapter Fifteen

Twas the night before Christmas....

Theodore's glee was uncontainable as he manned the loudspeaker system and unleashed his voice on the entire Toyland Compound.

Now they would know, once and for all, who was truly in control.

He imagined Kris's face and let that vision of defeat guide him as he spoke into the microphone.

"Yes, boys and girls, Maui was lovely, but I couldn't wait to get back to the land of peppermint sticks and gingerbread," he crooned. "So I'm back and I've come to take my rightful place. No room for pretenders to the throne, Kris, old fellow."

A hard edge came into his voice. "In fact, once this little operation is complete, I'm zapping the two humans right back to Colorado. Back to a time when they haven't met. Will never meet. There'll be no more threat from you two usurpers.

"But for now, all you need to know is this. I have the compound surrounded."

Not precisely true, but how could they know? Twelve strategically located elves with an adequate supply of Elfin Elixir could create the illusion of strength and give him the leverage he needed.

"I have you surrounded, and no one gets out until I get the key to the elixir storehouse." He paused to let that sink in, savoring the sound of the sharp, collective gasp that went up in the courtyard. "And the reins to the reindeer. That's all. That simple. Leave Christmas to me this year. Or there'll be no Christmas at all."

NICK CLASPED Virginia's hand tightly in his. He focused all his attention on the weary face of the bearded man sitting across from them at the kitchen table. Kris had just finished explaining who Theodore was. The maniacal elf planned to use the power of Christmas for his own gain, and not for the spread of peace and goodwill throughout the world. And from everyone's reaction, Theodore apparently had the power—and the black heart—to carry out all his threats.

Including his threat to ensure that Nick and Virginia had never met. Would never meet.

White-faced and nervous, Elsa bustled around, delivering hot chocolate to Kris, Noel, Virginia and Nick. Noel paced, toes alternately curling and uncurling. All waited for Kris to take charge.

But Kris looked defeated.

"I can't do it," he said at last, his mug of steaming, cinnamon-laced chocolate sitting untouched in front of him. "I'm too old for another round with Theodore."

"Oh, Kris, no!" Elsa put a hand on his, tears glistening in her blue eyes.

"He almost had me during the coup a few years back," Kris said, still staring into the steam from his cup. "I could never muster the energy now. Not at my age. The way the population's grown. All that electronic equipment I've had to haul around these last few years. It's done me in, I tell you. I'm not up to it."

Sensing the panic in Elsa's face and hearing the muffled cry from Noel, Nick looked at Virginia. He saw reflected there exactly what he was thinking.

It was up to them to save Christmas.

He watched as she drew a deep breath and turned to the three forlorn elves. "That's why Nick and I are here. We're not going to let Theodore spoil Christmas for the entire world."

Elsa's tears cleared. Noel stopped pacing, and his eyes returned to their normal shade of topaz. Even Kris looked up with a ray of hope shining in his eyes.

"You'd do that?"

Nick smiled at Virginia. "Isn't that why we're here?"

Instantly the gloomy meeting turned into a strategy session. Noel sprang onto the table and unrolled a map of the compound.

"My calculations indicate that Teddy can't have more than a dozen or so elves on his side this time," he said.

Kris shook his head. "But with enough Elfin Elixir, and knowing what they know about our flight plan..."

"Then we'll have to trip him up," Virginia said.

"Diversionary tactics," Nick agreed.

Noel clapped his hands gleefully. "Ooh, diversionary tactics. I like that. I like that. How do we do that, Nick?"

"Well, I don't know. If we could convince him somehow that Kris and the reindeer weren't going out as usual. Say they were leaving by some other route. Or at some other time than usual..." Nick's voice tapered off. He simply didn't know enough about the operation yet to be much help.

But Noel snapped his fingers with a tinkling sound. "The turbo-powered sleigh!"

Kris looked skeptical. "Are you sure it's ready, Noel? Seems to me there's still plenty of work to be done before we're sure it'll do the job."

"We don't have to use it," Noel said. "All we have to do is make Teddy *think* we're using it."

Elsa poured more chocolate into Nick's cup. "But how does it help to have Theodore think Kris is going out in the turbo-sleigh if we still have to get Dasher and Dancer and the rest off the ground?"

Nick spoke with quiet assurance. "Because he won't think it's Kris who's going out in the new sleigh. We'll tell him Virginia and I are making the run this year."

Virginia's eyes widened. "Us? Nick, we're not ready for that. We don't know a thing about how to handle

Christmas Eve. We'd botch the job and disappoint everybody just as surely as if Theodore were running the show."

"You've forgotten the operative word, Virginia." Her puzzled frown matched the others around the table. "Diversion."

Virginia's face blossomed into a smile. "Of course. New equipment. New flight plan. New crew."

Noel leapt five feet into the air. "And across the compound, while Teddy focuses his efforts on you two, Kris goes about business as usual! Brilliant!"

Kris laughed right out loud. "By jingle, I think that's just about perfect."

CHRISTMAS EVE WAS a frenzy of activity, as always. Only this time everything was done in duplicate. Bright red clothing, trimmed in fur, was pulled together like magic for Nick and Virginia. A fake pack was prepared. Much ado was made of preparing the turbo-sleigh, with enough fanfare to make sure that Theodore got wind of all that was going on.

And elsewhere, in quiet, with only Noel to help, Santa prepared the trusty sleigh and reindeer who had seen him through centuries of Christmases past.

In their room, after they changed into their festive clothing, Virginia sat on the bed they had shared and put her hand on her heart.

"Pounding like crazy," she said. "How silly. I'm as nervous as if I were actually going."

"Not silly," Nick said, taking her hands in his and pulling her up to stand beside him. "A lot is at stake here."

"If it doesn't work, what happens to us?"

"I don't know, Virginia. I honestly don't know."

"Right." She laughed nervously. "I'm not even sure I know what happens if we succeed."

With no sure answers to reassure her, Nick did all he knew to do. He took her in his arms and held her until the strength of their love gave them both courage to face the next few hours. And when they were once again filled with resolve, he put his hand in his pocket and retrieved a box he hadn't known was there until that very moment.

But when he saw the small gold-foil box with the iridescent red bow, an instinct in his heart told him exactly what to do with it.

"This is for you." He put the box in her reluctant hand. "Merry Christmas, Virginia."

She held the tiny box in both hands, feathering the ribbon with the side of her thumb. "Oh, Nick. And I haven't even—"

He pressed a finger lightly to her lips. "Shh. You will. Before it's over, you will."

She shrugged, her round face taking on a sheepish look that was disconcertingly familiar. It was some moments, while he watched her painstakingly unwrapping the box without tearing the paper, until he recognized that look.

It was the look of his kids in Sugarplum Bluff. The ones who weren't accustomed to getting presents; weren't entirely sure they deserved them. And didn't want to be too eager in case someone changed his mind.

Nick's heart turned over in his chest. A lifetime of gift giving wouldn't be enough to satisfy him that he had made up to Virginia all that she had missed in her girlhood.

Lying on a cloud of white in the tiny box was a gold-and-cloisonné locket. The moment Nick saw it, he felt a bolt of something magical strike at his heart. And Virginia must have felt the same, because she cried out softly when she saw the locket and put her hand to her heart.

"Nick. How... where...?" She looked up at him, tears in her eyes.

As much as he wanted to take credit for the gift, Nick knew he couldn't. "I think Santa took care of this one."

She touched the surface of the cameo gently, as if afraid it would disappear. "It's just like... like the one my mother had. Just like it."

A single tear trickled down her cheek. She looked up at him, the look in his eyes taking her breath away. "I guess Santa was just waiting for exactly the right gift giver."

Taking the cameo out of the box, she clicked open the locket, and all the color drained out of her face.

"Oh, Lord. Oh, Nick. This is like...it's like a dream. A miracle."

Putting his arm around her shoulder, Nick looked down. Two tiny faces smiled up at him from the locket—a light-haired man and a round-faced blond woman who looked like a 1960s version of the woman tucked under his arm.

"It's them, Nick. My mother and father." She looked up at him. "And I can...I can remember things. Things I haven't thought of in years. I remember my third birthday, when Mother made me a pink-and-white lace dress and Daddy made homemade ice cream. He held my hand and pretended to let me crank. And...and...the day we planted a tree in the front yard and Daddy said one day it would be taller than me and he put me on his shoulders to show me just how it felt to be that tall. And...and...everything. I remember all of it. Just as clearly as if...it might have happened yesterday." Tears were now streaming down her cheeks. "It's magic, isn't it?"

"Is that what you believe?"

She nodded.

"If you believe, that's exactly what it is, Virginia. Christmas magic."

MAGIC OR NO, Virginia was grateful she was only part of a scheme as she and Nick tucked themselves into the front of the sleek experimental sleigh. Her breath was coming in short spurts, and her heart skittered painfully beneath her rib cage.

"I'm not cut out for this much adventure, Closthaler," she said, unable to do a thing about the quaver in her voice. "Thank goodness all I'll really have to do is bake cookies and give the stamp of approval to baby dolls."

Elsa, who was tucking a blanket around her knees, clucked disapprovingly. "Now, now, Virginia. I believe it's time for Mrs. Claus—oh, I can't tell you how happy I was to hear that you two have decided to make everything nice and legal as soon as the rush is over. As I was saying, I believe the time has come for Mrs. Claus to take a much more active role. It's too big a job now for one man. The Santa of the future is going to need an equal partner, you know. I do believe that's one reason Kris selected you."

"Not because I'm short and blue eyed?" Virginia teased.

Elsa dimpled. "No, my dear, although that was certainly an asset in your favor. No, I believe he selected you because he knew you were a doer. And because... because you wanted a family so very much."

The two women shared a look, and Virginia impulsively reached out to hug Elsa. "Thank you."

Then Elsa backed away and went to join Kris, who was still fumbling with the bridle on the team of reindeer.

"I don't see Rudolph," Virginia murmured.

Nick smiled, checking out the controls he would have to learn by this time next year. "I think that's just a myth, Virginia."

And she laughed right out loud. "And how, Closthaler, am I supposed to tell the myths from the truths around here?"

At that moment, Noel clambered up the side of the sleigh and hung over the edge, pointing at a panel of buttons near Nick's left hand. "Now, that's the power. And there's automatic flight control. Gezochste-hagen—he's one of our most reliable elves—is in the control tower and he'll be in constant contact by radio. So all you have to worry about is—"

"Now, wait a minute, Noel. This is just diversionary, remember." Nick gestured to Kris, who was finally hoisting himself into the old-fashioned sleigh. "Kris is still the main man, don't forget."

"Oh. Right." And Noel smiled a secretive little smile that made the pounding of Virginia's heart pick up its pace once again.

And then it was time. Kris snapped his reins, and the team of reindeer began lumbering toward the runway. Noel gave the signal, and Nick hit the power switch.

"I'm almost sorry this isn't for real," Nick said as the turbo-powered sleigh started its breathtakingly swift ascent.

"Not me, Closthaler," Virginia said as the wind whirled gracefully through her hair. "I'll be a great little elf behind the scenes, but I'm still not so sure about all this flying."

Although, even as she said it, she realized she hadn't experienced the first moment of fear. It was almost as if she had never been afraid of flying.

As they hit an air pocket, the sleigh bumped slightly and the empty pack Noel had loaded into the sleigh as a decoy shifted and wedged against her back. Reaching back to move it, she realized the pack was suspiciously heavy and oddly lumpy. Peering into the top of the pack, she was stunned to realize it was filled with toys.

"Oh, no! Nick, stop! Noel screwed up. He put the wrong pack in with us. Kris's pack must be empty!"

"What? Wait, I'll have to..."

Then they both turned to look in the direction of the old-fashioned reindeer-powered sleigh as it reached the boundary of Toyland Compound and slowed, stalled by the shield Theodore's tiny band had fashioned using the last of their Elfin Elixir.

"Oh, no! It isn't working, Nick!" Virginia turned in her seat as they continued to soar forward, leaving Kris behind.

But as they shot through the night air, Kris waved his mittened hand and grinned. "I'm taking the night off! You two handle it, okay?"

Then they heard the angry wail that could only be Theodore realizing that he, too, had been duped.

Before anxiety could set in, Virginia felt Nick's hand wrap reassuringly around hers.

"I guess it's you and me, kid."

"They tricked us, too."

"Think of it as our little Christmas present to Kris and Elsa."

"But can we do it? We haven't been trained. We don't even have an itinerary. What if..."

Nick squeezed her hand. "Remember the children, Virginia?"

She did, and the memory calmed her. "I remember."

"Let's just follow the sound of the happiness in their hearts."

She sat back and relaxed, a smile forming on her lips as she stared at the confident profile of the man beside her. "It's coming through loud and clear, Nick."

And it was, although she did have a moment of worry that the happiness she heard was coming from her own heart. But as they soared through the night air, she realized it was all the same, this oneness of spirit that filled the air on a crisp, cool evening every December.

Epilogue

Happy Christmas to all...

One year and one day later, Virginia curled up against Nick's side, sighing in appreciation of the warmth from the fireplace on one side, her husband on the other and Noel's spiced cider on the inside. Her eyelids were heavy, and her muscles had the pleasant ache that comes from work well done.

"It was even better this year," she murmured, pressing her ear to the reassuring pump of Nick's heart.

"You're right," he said, and she heard the same satisfied weariness in his voice. "I think the best of all was Timmy Grafton. Did you see the look on his face?"

She smiled at the memory of the freckled face. "But did you feel what was in his heart?"

"You were right all along. He said he wanted a puppy, but what he really wanted was a baby sister."

"So by next year he'll have both. A woman knows these things."

They were just dozing off when the door to the study eased open and Noel stuck his pointy little nose around the corner. Virginia wanted to scowl, but she was too filled with good cheer to be grumpy to anyone, even someone who dared to disturb their long-overdue nap.

"Sorry, folks, but the mail just came in, and I thought you'd want to see this one." And he sailed a card through the air, projecting it to a perfect landing on Nick's lap before he backed out of the study and closed the door again.

Virginia picked up the card and held it up so they could both see it. "From Kris and Elsa!"

The front of the card was cheery with palm trees and waves and acres of silvery sand. On the back, in Elsa's careful script, it read:

Greetings from Miami. Kris has finally mastered surfing, and I haven't baked a cookie in three hundred and sixty-seven days! I'm into a size-nine bikini, and we both feel two hundred again. Congratulations on another good run. How about a two-week vacation in March, right before the factories crank up again? We've got a spare room, a spare surfboard, and we'd sure love a dozen fresh-baked gingerbread lifeguards, Virginia.

Love, E. and K.

Chuckling softly, Virginia looked up at Nick. "Are

you working as hard as I am to imagine Kris and Elsa on the beach in Miami?''

"Even with my imagination, it's a strain," he admitted. "But I'm getting used to straining."

The first year as official Mr. and Mrs. Claus had indeed been a strain, there was so much to learn and do. First order of business, at Elsa's insistence, had been the wedding, a simple affair held on New Year's Eve.

Noel and his crew had turned the compound courtyard into a winter wonderland. The snow glistened like diamonds beneath a moon as bright as a tropical sun— "It's strictly metaphysical, my dear," Elsa had explained, all seriousness as she pinned a lacy veil to Virginia's upswept hair. "Has to do with the reflected love in our hearts, or some such. Very mysterious. I've never understood all this stuff, to be perfectly honest." —and all the paths were strung with twinkling white lights and holly berries.

Wearing the white ermine robe that Elsa had been married in just centuries before, her hand resting in the crook of Kris's plump arm, Virginia had walked down the lane toward the candy-cane arch were Nick waited, resplendent in the sable robe that had also been handed down to the next generation.

"Is this real?" Virginia had whispered to Kris as they marched down the lane, which was lined with thousands of elves who could barely keep still and silent for the solemn moment. "I'm not going to wake up in the morning and find a lump of coal in my stocking, am I?''

Kris chuckled. ''Believe, my dear. That's all it takes to make it real.''

Then he had placed her hand in Nick's very solid, very real hand, and they spoke the powerful words of belief and trust and commitment that had kept the world on its steady course for more centuries even than Kris and Elsa had been handling the Christmas rush.

Nick's eyes had been bright with tears as he promised to cherish. Tears had threatened to shut down Virginia's voice, but nothing would keep her from promising to stand by him in sickness and in health.

They were the only ones who hadn't cried. Behind them, as Nick had raised the veil and bestowed a wondering kiss on the lips of the woman who was now his wife, Elsa had sniffled and Noel boo-hooed and Kris's belly had shaken like a bowl full of jelly—but not from laughter.

It had been the most beautiful, magical wedding Virginia had ever imagined, surrounded by her new, loving family.

The emotional intensity of the wedding had been followed by a few gripping weeks when Mother Nature had set up court at the North Pole and brought Theodore to justice. Virginia had thought that a lifetime sentenced to holding the San Andreas Fault together was a bit stiff, but she was glad to know Theodore wouldn't be haunting them again.

After that, a whirlwind training period had lasted
for a mere six weeks before Elsa put down her plump
little foot and insisted she and Kris pack for Miami.

If anything, their leavetaking had been even more
emotional than the wedding. While the elves turned
blue from trying so hard not to cry, and Elsa settled
into the sled that would take them out to Mother Nature's private jet, Kris had struggled to deliver a fare-
well speech to Toyland Compound.

"Now, my friends..."

Then he'd had to stop. He'd blown his nose.

"That is to say, I want you all to know..."

He'd stopped again, and made a great pretense of
wiping a speck from his eye.

"At any rate, you all know that through the
years..."

A sob had broken out way back in the ranks of the
elves. Kris's face had crumpled.

"Oh, blast it all, you'd better behave yourselves.
That's all I have to say. Because I'm still expecting to
know who's naughty and nice. So don't think you'll
get away with anything just because the old man's
gone. Blast it!"

And with the gruffest growl the jolly elf could muster, he'd dropped into his seat, grabbed the reins and
gave Dasher and Dancer one last nudge. And they
were gone.

Since then the elves had truly rallied behind their
new leaders. For at least two months, hardly a day
passed that Virginia didn't find tears welling up in her

eyes as her new family showered her with love. Hardly a day passed that she didn't look over at Nick and wonder just what she had done to deserve such happiness.

Yes, every day was Christmas in Virginia's new life. And if the look in Nick's eyes was any indication, he felt the same spirit of wonder himself.

Neither had forgotten to be grateful for all they had, even for a single day. Even throughout the most rigorous preparations leading up to the grand finale just two nights earlier.

And now, a short breather.

"If you'd known all this last year when I first climbed your mountain, would you have let the rock slide get me after all?"

"I think I did know it, somewhere deep inside."

She nodded; he had seemed to sense the importance of their mission long before she had. "I can't imagine a better Christmas. Or a better life."

"Next year," Nick vowed, "will be even better. I've got a lot of ideas for making next year even more special for all the children in the world."

He placed his hand against her belly. "And, of course, for one special child. The one you're carrying that will be ours alone."

AMERICAN ROMANCE®

Meet four of the most mysterious, magical men...in

MORE THAN MEN

In January, make a date with Gabriel...
He had a perfect body, honey-brown hair and sea-blue eyes, and when he rescued Gillian Aldair out of the crumbled mass of earth that was an Andes landslide, Gillian swore she'd never seen a man quite like him. But in her wildest imagination, she could never know just how different Gabriel was....

Join Rebecca Flanders for #517 **FOREVER ALWAYS**
January 1994

Don't miss any of the MORE THAN MEN titles!

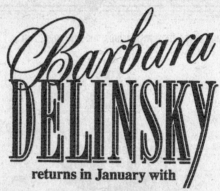

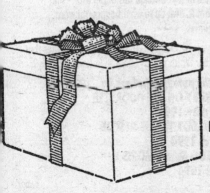

THE BABY IS ADORABLE...
BUT WHICH MAN IS HIS DADDY?

Alec Roman: He found baby Andy in a heart-shaped Valentine basket—
but were finders necessarily keepers?

Jack Rourke: During his personal research into Amish culture, he got close
to an Amish beauty—so close he thought he was the father.

Grady Noland: The tiny bundle of joy softened this rogue cop—and
made him want to own up to what he thought were
his responsibilities.

Cathy Gillen Thacker brings you TOO MANY DADS, a three-book series that
asks the all-important question: Which man is about to become a daddy?

Meet the potential fathers in:
#521 BABY ON THE DOORSTEP
February 1994
#526 DADDY TO THE RESCUE
March 1994
#529 TOO MANY MOMS
April 1994

DADS

Relive the romance...
Harlequin® is proud to bring you

by Request™

A new collection of three complete novels every month. By the most requested authors, featuring the most requested themes.

Available in January:

WESTERN LOVING

They're ranchers, horse trainers, cowboys...
They're willing to risk their lives.
But are they willing to risk their hearts?

Three complete novels in one special collection:

RISKY PLEASURE by JoAnn Ross
VOWS OF THE HEART by Susan Fox
BY SPECIAL REQUEST by Barbara Kaye

Available wherever Harlequin books are sold.

My Valentine
1994

Celebrate the most romantic day of the year with
MY VALENTINE 1994
a collection of original stories, written by
four of Harlequin's most popular authors...

MARGOT DALTON
MURIEL JENSEN
MARISA CARROLL
KAREN YOUNG

*Available in February, wherever
Harlequin Books are sold.*

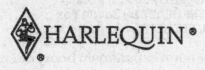

HARLEQUIN ®